SARA
WHEN SHE
CHOOSES

CAT JENKINS

SARA
WHEN SHE
CHOOSES

Dragonfeather Books
Bedazzled Ink Publishing Company • Fairfield, California

978-1-945805-65-3 paperback

Cover Design
by

DESIGNS

Dragonfeather Books
a division of
Bedazzled Ink Publishing, LLC
Fairfield, California
http://www.bedazzledink.com

For Shelly and Sue, my literary soul-sisters

and for Dennis, who calls me Sara . . .

1

SARA HATED EVERYTHING about Granny's house.

From the chunks of clay with symbols scratched into them that clattered in the breeze where they hung from the porch rafters, to the coarse pallets stuffed with Spanish moss that were supposed to be beds, to the murky bayou water that oozed all about the cabin and what passed for its yard, Sara hated it all.

Granny's house was more of a shack, really. It was built on top of massive, old stumps to keep it dry when the water would rise, but it still had a greeny-damp kind of odor that got into your clothes and hair. Sara said she could still smell Granny's place for weeks after one of her visits.

"That's *mold*," Amy-Dean, Sara's big sister, would interject into her complaints with a sniff of superiority. "Mold and *mildew*!"

"Greeny-damp!" Sara would insist. She never liked losing arguments, especially to Amy-Dean.

When Sara was seven years old, Granny had sent for her. Mama said Granny needed her to "help out for a spell." Sara protested that neither Amy-Dean nor her brother Michael had to leave all *their* friends and travel to some swamp to help an old lady they never saw or heard from any other time of the year. It wasn't as though Sara was the only girl or the eldest. It was just dumb, bad luck, she thought. Mama tried to make it sound as though it were an honor, but Sara could tell that something about it worried her. At times she even thought it scared Mama a little.

"Granny says it's got to be you. So, Sara-Jean Mayhew, you mind your manners and do what Granny tells you. It's only for two weeks. You'll have all the rest of the summer to waste time with your friends."

Late at night Sara thought she heard harsh whispering coming from her parents' room. Mama and Papa were arguing, and Sara's name popped up too often, but in the end, Mama packed Sara's bag and drove her all the way to Chalmette where Granny stood on the shore waiting for them.

Sara, already in a resentful mood, really didn't want to go any further when she saw that frizzy white hair, and that shapeless old dress, and the chipped-up, leaky rowboat that Granny said was their ride.

Mama loaded her bag into the boat.

Granny took her hand. "Don't fret, child. You might find yourself some wonders while you're here. Just keep your eyes and mind open."

Granny pulled on the oars and gained momentum through the rush-choked waters. Mama waved from the bank, getting smaller and smaller.

Sara let the anger and rebellion seething inside her grow as the little boat slipped deeper and deeper into the bayou. It didn't help when they finally tied up to a tree alongside Granny's watery back yard, and Sara lugged her bag toward the porch, bumping it loudly up the steps, that Granny put her face down close to Sara's.

"Shhhhhhhh . . . Careful with that bag. You don't want to be wakin' any ghosts now, do you, child?" She laughed loud enough to rouse the dead herself.

Sara didn't laugh at all.

Sara was in for two weeks of bored misery. No electricity, no TV, no phone, no wireless, not even any books Sara wanted to read. To be fair, Granny did have some good stories to tell in the evenings, but Sara was determined to make sure her grandmother knew how miserable she was, so she kept her head down and didn't let on when she was interested. She hoped that if she were truly unpleasant company, Granny would send her home early and never invite her back.

The only thing Granny asked her to do every day was take a big, wooden bucket down to what she called "the river" and bring it back filled with water. Since the same slimy, murky water eddied almost right up alongside the house, Sara didn't see why she had to pick her way through the tussocks and pools to this one particular river place. When she asked, Granny just told her to do it with her mind and eyes open. It seemed to Sara that her grandmother really didn't need help at all. Sara became suspicious as the days passed, since "helping out" was why she thought she had been sent for in the first place.

A week and a half into her stay, Sara couldn't stand it anymore. That evening, as she watched her grandmother rocking methodically in her old cedar chair on the porch, she broke her sullen silence.

"Granny, why did you want me to come here? I haven't helped you with anything, except fetching water that you don't need. Why am I here?"

"You're here to see the laputa bird, child." Granny's rocking kept on in its steady rhythm.

Sara tried again after a long silence.

"What's a laputa bird? Tell me what it's like and I'll look for it."

Granny stopped rocking, turned, and peered through the darkening dusk for a long, slow moment at Sara. "You'll know when you see it." She resumed rocking.

"Why didn't you ask Michael or Amy-Dean to come here?"

"'Cause those two for sure will never see the laputa. You might not either, girl, but I'm a-bettin' you will."

That was all Sara could find out that first year. She was jubilant when the two weeks were up and Granny rowed them both back to meet Mama.

Granny gave her head the tiniest shake and Mama's anxious, inquiring look turned to one of relief, but Sara didn't really notice; she was that glad to be headed home.

The next summer it was the same thing. Only this time Sara knew what was in store for her and made even more of a fuss about going.

"Only two weeks out of your whole year, Sara-Jean. It makes your Granny happy to see you. How can you be so selfish? Just go and show her the respect she's due. She's *my* Mama, after all."

Sara's mother didn't give an inch. Her father kept quiet, but looked a bit thunderous about the brow. Her brother and sister snickered at her whenever they thought their parents wouldn't notice.

Because youngest daughters in Sara's family were powerless to decide things like when they'll go to bed or what they'll eat for dinner or where they'll spend the summer, the visits to Granny became a dreaded routine.

When Sara was nine she asked Granny how much longer she'd need to come to "help out." Dark eyes glinting in the glow shed by the kerosene lamp, Granny gave her the long, slow regard she'd come to expect.

"Once you see the laputa bird, you don't have to come back no more, lessin' you want to."

"There're lots and lots of birds around, Granny. Maybe I've already seen it," Sara offered with a hopeful, but disingenuous smile.

"No. When you see it, you'll know." Granny gazed out into the bayou blackness, the way she did every night. "I'll know, too," she added.

Sara thought it sounded ominous.

"What's so special about this luh-laputa bird?"

The silence lasted so long, Sara wondered if she'd been heard, but Granny was just thinking, considering which words would be best to turn the knob of a door that maybe wasn't ready to be opened yet. Strengthening her resolve that she had *not* invited this sullen child to her home in vain, she decided to answer . . . just a little.

"If you see the laputa bird, it'll mean our blood is still runnin' true. It'll mean you can take the world your mama chose out city-way, *or* you can come here and learn the swamp-works like I know, and my mama knew, and her mama before her, and back before ever there was a city could steal a girl away. See the laputa and you'll be able to hear the bayou lullaby. See the laputa and you'll have a choice to make."

Sara didn't really understand, but it shivered her skin just the same.

Another summer passed, Sara's tenth, and she could tell Granny might be starting to have some doubts. Sara had resigned herself to the two week interruptions in her regular life, but a thrill of anticipation shot through her anyway. If Granny gave up, she might not want her there anymore and she'd be free. Sara was surprised to discover a little corner of her would miss Granny and her quaint, creepy home. But she comforted herself with the thought that maybe they could bring her grandmother inland to Sara's house instead for a yearly visit.

That hope made Sara's eleventh summer, her fifth visiting Granny, a little easier to take. By now Sara didn't hide that Granny's stories, told on the porch in the sultry night air, caught her interest. She could even admit that there was a disheveled kind of beauty in the swamp. She still didn't like the murky, brown water, though. She always felt as though something was hiding, lurking in it; something that was keeping secrets or concealing crimes.

But even the strangest things could become normal if you had to confront them on a regular basis. So Sara didn't think twice anymore when Granny asked her to fetch water, as she'd been doing every day for every visit for every summer since she was seven.

Even with the tricky tides, she could now pick her way easily over to "the river." So this unremarkable day in this un-special visit, she crouched down on one of the firmer mounds of reeds and swung the familiar bucket down into the feeble current. She watched the brown-gray water slowly gurgle its way over the thick, wooden rim. "Sluggish" was the word Sara favored when describing to herself how the water around Granny's place moved. Now, as she waited for the bucket to fill, she hummed the word to herself, like the melody of a secret little rebellion against this chore she saw as useless.

"Sluggish," she breathed as the scum and small swamp-life circled itself into rounded patterns on the water's surface.

"Sluggish," she murmured as her eyes grew unfocused with boredom while she dipped the bucket a little lower to speed things along.

"Slug . . . gish."

Sara blinked. Her scream echoed through the bayou.

Granny heard her all the way back at the cabin. She stopped harvesting swamp-greens for a moment and smiled. A deep sigh of relief that had been pent up inside her for long years broke loose.

Half an hour later, Sara dragged herself up the porch steps, panting, slimed from hip to heel. The bucket was empty and dripping.

Granny smiled. "I'm thinkin' you saw the laputa bird, girl. I hoped you would."

Sara closed her eyes and could still see them. Mottled toad-brown and frog-green. Eyes like oily rainbows. Wings outstretched. Flying fast. Beneath the water. Making a clicking sound that had seemed to echo Sara's breathy, little hum.

"I guess you got some choices to make now," Granny said as she spread the swamp-greens she had harvested out to dry. "But I'm a-bettin' you'll need another look at the laputa. That's how it usually goes. If you're agreeable. If the blood runs true."

Sara plopped onto one of the old hewn-wood chairs, bucket still gripped in her white-knuckled hands, mud and marsh-goo drying on her clothes and skin.

"Tell me about the blood, Granny." Her voice creaked faint and rusty.

"Surely, child, but we'll be needin' some water first." Her smile was warm as she raised an eyebrow at the empty bucket. "You don't have to go back to the river. You can fill it right here off'n the back deck. Water is water, after all."

2

THAT EVENING SARA picked at her boiled greens and fresh catfish fried in crispy butter. She couldn't get the laputa bird out of her thoughts. It jumped and swirled and swam, claiming all her focus. When she judged Granny was done eating and ready to take her place in the old rocking chair on the porch, the way she did every night, Sara knew the time was right.

"What were they, Granny? I saw them, but . . . what were they?" The dark, muggy air seemed to draw in closer, as though it wanted to hear the answer, too.

"The laputa? Why, it's a harbinger, child."

"A harbinger?"

"That's right. A harbinger is like an introduction, tellin' of things to come."

Sara frowned. "A harbinger of what?"

Granny rocked in a slow, methodical rhythm, her gaze darting about as if she were following the movements of things in the swamp and the thick, night air. Sara had often wondered about Granny's active eyes. Even when she'd be telling her stories, her eyes were never still. Sara had decided it was just one of those things old folks did; some peculiarity that she rather hoped she'd never understand. Not first-hand, anyway. Now she wondered if there was more to it than that. Now she wondered what other strange creatures might live unseen in Granny's bayou.

"Laputa is a harbinger of knowledge."

"What knowledge?"

"Knowledge of the truth of things. Understandin' of the power that the Deep Places have to offer."

"But that's just it! I *don't* understand, Granny." Sara wanted a simple answer. She wanted to hear that that underwater bird was some rare, strange species that no one had officially discovered yet. She wanted to hear that it wasn't a bird at all; just some kind of odd, sort of musical fish. She most definitely did *not* want to hear that it was the beginning of something. Especially when that something made her skin shudder and bump in a cold, shivery way.

"Anything I tell you now, child, won't mean much." Granny sighed. "The understandin' will come in its own time." She focused intently on Sara. "But nothing will come at all if you decide you don't want to go any further."

"But . . ."

"No buts, girl. The next thing you have to do is choose. Do you want to learn more, or do you want to return to your home and your family full time? No more summer visits. Or do you want to learn the swamp-works, like me, and my mama before that, and so on and so on back to the Beginnin'?"

"I don't even know what that means, Granny. Beginning of what? Beginning when and where?" Sara was having a hard time figuring out where all this was headed. She felt as though she'd suddenly become an exchange student in her own life. Words that had nice, solid, comfortable meanings had been turned strange, foreign, and ungraspable. Sara pulled her knees up to her chin and squinched in on herself to become as small and tight and safe as possible.

All this talk about choices was hard. So far in her young life Sara hadn't been allowed to make many choices at all. Everything had been decided for her based on what her parents thought was best, or on the pecking order between her and Amy-Dean and Michael. The only time Sara got to make a choice about anything was when it wasn't important or didn't seem to matter to anyone else.

The choice Granny was talking about sounded as though it would matter a great deal, and not just to Sara, but to everyone. It sounded big. Too big for her—a small, plain girl—to choose correctly, or choose right *now*!

Granny sensed the turmoil raging through Sara. "Don't fret, child," she said in soothing tones. "You don't need to speak tonight. You'll be here a few more days yet. Just keep your eyes and your mind open."

Granny creaked her way out of her rocking chair, glanced once more at Sara, then made her way across the old porch and through the front door to prepare for bed.

Sara could hear her tossing the leavings from their dinner off the back deck for the fish and 'gators to feed on, and then washing dishes in the big, galvanized bucket filled with soapy water kept for just that task. The clinking and clanking finally stopped and it sounded as though Granny had settled into her big, Spanish moss bed. Sara sighed, unfolded herself, and went inside, too.

There were no mirrors in Granny's house, which had made Sara uncomfortable at first when she had to brush her teeth or hair. But tonight it didn't matter at all. Her mind was a whirlwind of worry, confusion, and an excited kind of thrill, too. As she dipped a dented, tin cup into the boiled-water barrel to rinse her teeth, she was struck by how, in a heartbeat, Granny's house, nestled in the swamp, had become the *least* boring place she'd ever been.

Sara brushed her normally straight, brown hair. She ran her hand down its length on one side, feeling a little wave and frizz that was only there during her time in the humid air of the swamp. Pulling a lock in front of her eyes, she wondered for a moment what it looked like here. Once, during her first visit, she'd complained and demanded to know why Granny couldn't have even a tiny shard of a mirror just to help a girl keep herself neat. Granny had looked at her as though she were announcing the sky had cracked in two.

"Mirrors are only reflections," was her cryptic reply. "If things go the way I hope, you'll be learnin' to see the *real*, not the image."

Sara let go of her hair. She dropped the hand holding the brush to her side. Seeing the laputa bird chased her thoughts around and around, sending them off to places they'd never been before. *If* the laputa hadn't flown (swum?) by just as she was filling the old bucket, *if* it had been there all along, that would mean that the change was in Sara, in how she was seeing things. Could that be what Granny had meant all these years about keeping her eyes open?

She put her hairbrush down on the heavy, wooden plank that served as a kitchen counter. With careful, measured steps she walked to the window overlooking the back deck. She peered out into the night and felt the breath rush from her lungs. She gripped the windowsill to keep herself steady. For an instant it felt as though the whole cabin tilted beneath her feet.

Something *was* different!

Sara had seen the swamp at night plenty of times. She'd seen it in the rain, the wind, under a full moon, and in deep darkness when only starlight touched the foliage with faint, cold silver. She'd rarely been able to make out any details beyond the strange, dark trees with leaves like black holly that surrounded Granny's shack, or the long, dank skeins of Spanish moss dripping onto the sodden ground. Now she looked out on a bayou grown alien.

A faint, pearly-green glow picked out the features of the terrain with a delicate, sparkling grace. It wasn't intense or bright, but it trapped Sara's breath with its strangeness.

"Granny? GRANNY!!" she called, unable to look away from the eerie landscape.

"Hmmmpff? Wha'?" Sara could hear her grandmother's muffled, sleep-dulled voice and the rustling of the moss as she heaved herself to a sitting position to see what all the ruckus was about.

"Granny! Everything's different! There're lights in the swamp all of a sudden! What is it?"

Granny craned her neck and looked toward Sara standing before the back deck window. "Oh, that," she grumbled in what Sara considered an inappropriately calm response. "Go to sleep, girl. Nothin' there in the night that weren't there in the day. We'll talk more in the mornin'."

With that, Granny plumped her moss-and-lichen pillow, pulled her threadbare blanket up to her chin, and curled herself into a comfortable position facing the wall.

After a few moments, Sara realized that staring and blinking and rubbing her eyes wasn't helping anything. She padded to her bed on the far side of the cabin and huddled beneath her own blanket, keeping a wary eye on the greenly glistening bit of swamp visible through the window.

After a time, that watchful eye blinked longer and slower, until it closed on its own.

ॐ

SARA WOKE THE next morning and heard Granny bustling about as usual, boiling water for chicory bark tea, grilling salted bacon, and cooking a large pot of cinnamon oatmeal over the coals in the gray stone fireplace. Sara snuggled down deeper into her bedding, happy to doze for a few more minutes before Granny called her to breakfast.

Like an explosion, memories of the previous day . . . and night! . . . came tumbling and crashing from wherever memories hide when one is sleeping. Her eyes flew open, and she bolted upright, whisking locks of unruly hair out of her eyes. Had it been real? Was she just now waking from one of those dreams that slips its way into the daylight world to make getting out of bed a very confusing business indeed?

No. The laputa birds. The swamp etched in pearly-pale light. It had happened. It was real.

With caution born of wonder Sara craned her neck so she could see as much of the swamp as possible through the back deck window without actually leaving the security of her bed. As far as she could see it looked normal: gray and green and dank, punctuated by those weird black holly trees that grew close by the cabin, but nowhere else.

Granny noticed Sara taking in the view and chuckled as she ladled oatmeal into two deep, wooden bowls.

"Rise and shine, girl. I 'spect you've got a passel of questions, and answers won't be comin' to anyone who stays in bed. We've a busy day before us. Get'cha up. Get'cha up."

It was beyond Sara to comprehend how Granny could be so unendingly cheerful when the whole world (meaning Sara's view of it) had undergone such a radical change. But she knew the only way to figure it all out was to do as Granny said and get'cha up. So, a little resentful and a lot curious, Sara dressed quickly and took her place across from her grandmother at the knotted pine table that almost filled the kitchen area.

Despite the previous day's upsets, she found she now had a hearty appetite and was grateful to savor a few spoonfuls of oatmeal and a slice of bacon before slowing her pace long enough to ask the first of what she felt would be an endless ocean of questions.

"Granny, what's happening to me? Did you see the swamp last night? What's this all about? What's it mean? Can other people see the same things, like the laputa bird? Were they always there? If they were, why didn't I see them before?"

"Whoa there, child. I'll tell you what you want to know when you need to know it, but one question at a time, girl. Now finish up your breakfast, and we'll go for a walk out bayou-way." Granny turned her full attention to her second cup of chicory bark tea.

Sara sensed it wouldn't do any good to keep peppering her with questions, no matter how dire she felt the need to know *now*. So she gulped down the rest of her meal in a feverish hurry, helped Granny clean up, and fidgeted about on the front porch as Granny took her time putting on what she referred to as her "walkabout clothes." These were chiefly drab and careworn and seemed to include a number of rubberized, waterproofed items like boots, pocket-liners, and an unflattering pouch with a mysteriously lumpy appearance.

At last, Granny was satisfied with her preparations and walked out onto the porch where Sara was doing a poor job of disguising her increasing impatience.

Granny stopped on the top step, sniffed the air and stretched in appreciation of the day.

Sara could contain herself no longer. "Come *on*, Granny!" she blurted in frustration.

Granny trained calm regard on Sara who was sure it was a deliberate attempt to set an example of superior patience and maturity. "What was the first thing I ever told you when you came to me, child?"

Sara didn't even have to pause to think. "To keep my eyes and my mind open?"

"That's right. Now your eyes are open. But if you want your mind to follow, you're goin' to have to pay attention and take things at their own pace . . . meanin' *my* pace when it comes to answers . . . and not the pace *you* think things should go. Now. Follow me."

Sara did as she was told, feeling slightly humbled.

It didn't take long to see that they were headed down to the place where Sara had seen the laputa birds the day before. Had it only been yesterday? She felt as though too much had been crammed into those few short hours. It seemed like days, or even weeks should have passed.

As they approached "the river," Sara plucked up her nerve to ask questions again, but determined she'd do it a little more selectively and only one at a time.

"Granny?"

"Hmmmmm?"

"When I first came to you, you said you weren't interested in Amy-Dean or Michael. What made you think I was different?"

"An old photograph."

A thousand more questions streaked through Sara's mind on as many different tangents, but she took a deep breath as they picked their way from tussock to tussock and selected just one.

"How did an old photo do that?"

Granny grinned to herself in appreciation of Sara's restraint. "When you were born, your mama was real proud, but she was also real busy, what with three young'uns to look after all at once. One day she was cleanin' out your garage and she found an old camera. Not one of those fancy computer ones I hear tell of these days, but a real relic.

"Well, she saw that old thing had some film in it and she were curious to see if'n it'd still work. So, she had your brother and sister hold you between them and she snapped herself a few pictures. She sent me one. I still have it tacked up by the cooler-box. Noticed it, have ye?" Granny gave Sara a sharp glance with her piercing black eyes before returning to the careful trail they were following.

Sara remembered seeing the photo, but she hadn't paid it much mind. She was so little in it—not even one year old—that she didn't recognize herself. And she wasn't much interested in pictures of Amy-Dean and Michael. In her opinion there were far too many of those around as it was. Mama and Papa said it was just because her siblings were older and had been around longer; more photo-ops, but Sara felt slighted anyway.

"I saw that old picture, Gran, but I didn't notice anything unusual," Sara admitted.

"You take a look at it again when we get back, now that your eyes are open. What you'll see is what gave me hope that our blood was still runnin' true, still survivin' for at least another gen'ration."

They reached what Granny generously termed "the river" and stopped a few feet from the shore. Noticing the disgruntled look on Sara's face, Granny shook her head and chuckled to herself.

"I guess I've 'bout forgotten what it's like to be young and needin' answers. Okay, girl. I'll tell you, and you can see for yourself this evenin' back at the cabin.

"You know how those new-fangled, computery cameras all have that way of keepin' people's eyes from showin' red? Well, this old camera your mama used didn't have anythin' like that. So when she sent me the picture of the three of you, I noticed right off. Amy-Dean and Michael have those pesky red-dot eyes. But you, Sara-Jean, your eyes shone bright and glowin' silvery-green. Same as an ocelot or a swamp fox."

Sara wasn't sure she understood. Her eyes were brown. Sure, if you got them in the light at just the right angle and looked very, very closely, you could pick out bits of gray and olive green. But for everyday purposes they were plain, old brown. Amy-Dean, who had inherited Papa's clear, blue color, never let Sara forget the "plain old" part when describing the traits handed down to her younger sister.

Granny continued. "Do you see, child? Everyone gets red-dot eyes. You have silver-green-dot eyes."

It was all a bit too undefined for Sara. She thought that "plain old" was maybe a good thing sometimes. Especially when applied to explanations.

"So how did silver-green-dot eyes make you think there was something special about me?" she persisted.

Granny looked up at the Spanish moss trailing from all the limbs of the trees like pale celadon icicles. She looked at the sulfurous lime areas of lichens and mosses rendering boulders and tree trunks into patchwork quilts. She noted the faint emerald sheen rippling across the slow-flowing water before them. Finally, she turned back to Sara.

Voice low and reverent, she said, "Take a look around, child. A thousand shades of green you'll never see anywhere else. Green is a sacred color here in the swamp. Green is the color of Power. For those born into it, green is Destiny. That's why I asked your mama to send you to me. That's why your mama agreed to give you a chance. To find out if you *have* a choice."

And there it was again; the queer, jumpy, scared-but-eager feeling in Sara's stomach whenever she came up against this choice she was supposed to make.

4

IN THE WAKE of Sara's silence, Granny turned back toward the river and stepped out onto the edge of the bank, indicating Sara should follow her. Sara did so, but kept her eyes fixed on the ground around her feet. She wasn't sure she was ready to see a laputa bird again. Not just yet. She wanted to take a few breaths and digest what Granny had told her about the meaning of green.

"Look, child," Granny said, after a few moments. "Look at the current."

By slow increments Sara raised her eyes from her muddy sneakers to the yellowish reeds and grasses growing down to the water's edge and, finally, to the water itself moving in gentle ripples. To her relief, there wasn't a dizzying flock of fowls racing below the surface; no chiming, clicking birdsong. But as she gazed into the depths, mesmerized, she did see an occasional, lone, oily-eyed creature flitting by, almost like an eerie assurance that such things did exist after all. She held her breath and listened, but there was no mocking echo of a melody. Of course, Sara wasn't humming this time. She wondered if that made a difference.

"Notice anything?" Granny's head was bent toward the river, but her bright, sidelong glance prodded Sara to look more closely at the water, rather than what might be traveling through it. As far as the surface and the current went, everything looked exactly the same as it had every day Sara had come to fill the old bucket for the last few years.

"Which way do you reckon is the ocean?" Granny prompted.

Sara squinted up at the cloudy sky. After her first invitation to the swamp when she was seven, she had taken a careful look at a map showing the whole area. She recalled how impressed she'd been with the tremendous size of the bayou, and that the ocean was south. Which meant . . .

Sara caught her breath in a sharp, audible gasp. "The river's not running toward the ocean!"

"That's right, child. It's not."

Sara felt that queasy feeling in her stomach again. This couldn't be right. Even only being in the sixth grade, she knew that rivers run toward the nearest ocean or some other larger body of water unless something was done to alter their natural course. Somehow, she didn't think civilization had encroached on this watery wilderness enough to account for a river running northeast when it should be headed south. And water was everywhere. She didn't recall any particular body of water on the map other than the sea.

"Then where's it going?" she asked, feeling perturbed, as though the current were exerting effort to confound her like a sly, untrustworthy frenemy.

"Someplace I've never rightly been myself," Granny murmured, "though I'd surely like to see it with my own eyes."

She straightened from bending toward the river. The look she gave and the grave tone of her voice told Sara to pay rapt attention.

"The current here flows toward the Source. You recall my mention of the Deep Places, do you, girl?"

Sara nodded.

"Well, there are a number of Deep Places on this old Earth. You'll find them where fire or water hold sway. Now I never have heard of anyone tryin' to find themselves a path into a volcano to reach a Deep Place, but there have been some who try to get to the Source of the watery kind." She lifted her chin higher and gazed in a northeasterly direction. "Some go lookin' and never come back. Hard to say if they found the Source and didn't want to leave, or if they got waylaid and never made it. Hard to say." Granny stared out at the water, seeming lost in her own reckonings.

"What's the Source?" Sara asked.

Granny shook herself out of her thoughts and back to the present. "The Source is where the Deep Place in these parts comes to the surface. Learn the swamp-works and the Source will be what gives you Knowledge and Power. That's what flows *out* of the Source."

Granny walked on, Sara following on her heels. They picked their way deeper into the bayou than Sara had ever been. After a while, she judged that she could hazard another question without irritating her grandmother.

"Have *you* ever tried to reach the Source?"

Granny kept her eyes on the marshy ground as she answered. "Yep. I did give it a try a time or two."

Somehow the answers were never informative enough for Sara. But she had always been taught that persistence was a virtue, if done with consideration and if not carried too far.

"What kept you from reaching it?"

"Well, things get stranger and stranger the closer you get to the Source. I guess I figur'd the journey was too risky just to slake a yen to know. I have a job to do here on the fringes of the Power, and I reckoned I could do it without havin' to see what I already knew was there. Besides, if anythin' happened to me, there would've been no one to take my place, seein' as your mama chose a city way of life." A grin lit up her face as she looked back over her shoulder at Sara. "But now you're here, and mayhap that might make up for losin' my own girl. Dependin' on what you choose, of course."

They trudged on in silence, the sounds of wildlife and the watery landscape keeping them company. The day grew warmer and muggier. Sara was getting hungry and was just about to suggest they turn back when Granny stopped. They were at the edge of a cliff, which surprised Sara. She'd always thought of the entire bayou as flatland, but now she realized that part of her discomfort was due to the fact that for some time they'd been walking up a gentle incline.

Granny looked about for a solid place to sit and gestured for Sara to join her on a large, sloping boulder a few feet back from the cliff's edge. She rummaged about in the lumpy pouch she had tied to her waist that morning. Sara's stomach gave a grateful rumble when Granny produced two sandwiches made from leftover breakfast bacon and an antique-looking bottle filled with tepid water which they shared between them.

Lunch was accomplished in restful quiet, the sound of munching precluding much in the way of talk. After they finished, Granny stowed the water bottle back in her pouch, stood, and motioned for Sara to accompany her closer to the cliff's edge.

"Do you see anythin' down there, girl?"

Sara had a healthy respect for heights and was careful not to get too close to what she now saw was an undercut embankment. For the second time that day, she gasped, squeezing the breath out of her. For a moment her lungs felt paralyzed by the sight below.

Far down from where they stood, the familiar brown-gray waters continued to flow on their unnatural course away from the ocean. Caught up in the current, floating at random intervals were glowing, pastel shapes like large, fuzzy lozenges. Sara noted rosy pink, glowing lavender, translucent ivory, celadon green, pale blue, and creamy orange. There was no pattern to this odd migration, and although the number of shapes passing by did seem to ebb and flow, their movement was steady and continuous.

"What are they?" she breathed; her whisper as hushed as would befit a place demanding awe.

"They're what flows *into* the Source," came Granny's soft reply. "Some say they're life essences, souls. And I believe them."

"Souls?! Like . . . like *people*?" Sara choked out in horror.

"I suppose. If'n someone wanders into the swamp and dies there. That does happen some." Clearly Granny didn't share Sara's abhorrence of the idea. She spoke with respect, almost, Sara thought, with longing. "But mostly they're the essence of things that live their whole lives here and just pass on. Birds, fish, 'gators, snakes, trees, moss . . . all the life of the swamp."

"Plants?" Sara questioned. She had a hard time putting a handful of Spanish moss on equal footing with animals or, if her grandmother were to be believed, maybe even the occasional wayward person.

"Why surely, child. This place is full of life. Most of it you never see or take note of. But everythin' livin' has that spark of somethin' that makes it special. When that spark is set free around here, it finds its way back to the Source, takin' all it knows, all it's learned with it." She dragged her gaze away from the rainbow colors traveling in silence below them to give Sara a good, long look. "Most people can't see them, girl. Even after seein' the laputa bird, most folks can't see that much more for weeks, sometimes years, sometimes ever. You're seein' way more, way faster than anyone I ever knew. Shouldn't have seen the pearl-glow for some time yet. But you did. And now you see them that travels. It'd be a right shame if you didn't . . ." She caught herself, pressing her lips tight as she looked at Sara.

To Sara's further discomfort, she thought she saw tears gathering in the corners of Granny's eyes. She couldn't be sure. It was just a hint of prism-sparkle, but then Granny straightened up, stepped back, and announced in a brisk tone that it was time to return to the cabin.

Sara found it hard to tear herself away from the stately movement of the glowing shapes below them, but at Granny's repeated insistence about going home, she managed to turn away and leave them to their strange journey.

6

FOR THE FIRST part of the trek back Sara was uncharacteristically quiet. She reflected that, although some questions had been answered, a great many more had popped up to replace them. The sun had set by the time they reached the cabin, but they had no trouble finding a dry path. The faint green illumination that had so startled Sara the night before limned every tree and puddle, every beard of moss, and every leaf. If anything, the pale glow was a tiny bit brighter, Sara thought.

As they hopped from tussock to tussock to gain the front porch, Sara stopped, looking from side to side and top to bottom. "Granny, what is this green light? It wasn't here before last night, was it?"

Continuing her progress toward the porch steps, Granny replied, "I reckon what you're seein' is one of the gifts the Source gives those born to the blood; to keep them a bit safer if they have to travel by night. And I reckon it's always been there. You just couldn't see it until your eyes were opened."

With that, she pulled herself up onto the porch, gave a deep, weary sigh, and moved toward the front door. "Now, no more questions for the moment, girl. Let's get us cleaned up and have some supper. Then we'll talk a bit more."

As Granny pulled off her boots and went inside Sara could hear her muttering to herself, "Land sakes! I'm gettin' too old for these swamp hikes. And I bet that girl's gonna have a dozen things she wants to know 'fore we can call it a day. Land sakes!"

But once the mud had been washed off and a tasty dinner of crawfish stew and honeyed cornbread had been consumed, Granny settled herself in her usual place on the porch, looking into the night gathered in thick drifts of dark about the cabin. Sara sat on the top porch step, her knees drawn up so she could rest her chin on them as her mind whirled with all the strange, new things she'd been privy to for the past two days. It was difficult to know where to start, even with her grandmother apparently resigned to a good, long question-and-answer session. Sara took a deep breath and dove in.

"So you've lived here in the swamp your whole life. Right, Granny?"

"Yes, child."

"And it's because you were somehow born into it, and I'm supposed to be the same way?"

"That's right. The fact that you can see laputas, the swamp-glow at night, and the travelin' souls I showed you today make it a sure thing, not a guess."

"But what do you *do* out here, Granny? All these gifts, or talents, or whatever they are . . . what do you *do* with them?"

Granny's voice was gentle, keeping time with the rhythmic rocking of her chair. "I work to keep the Balance, child. People like us are needed to keep the Source fit. I know that doesn't mean much right now, but, goin' the rate you are, you'll feel it soon enough . . . Maybe too soon," she added like a private aside to herself; the words touched with a hint of uncertainty.

Sara let out a small, gusty breath of dissatisfaction. "I don't get it, Gran."

Granny stopped rocking and, placing her elbows on her knees, leaned toward Sara where she huddled on the steps.

"If you understand nothin' else, girl, understand this: the Source is very, very powerful. So powerful it affects things way far beyond the swamp. When the Source is balanced and runnin' the way it should, things in the world run the way *they* should. But sometimes it happens that the Source gets pushed off course. It gets all out of kilter. That's when bad things start to happen.

"I'm not sayin' anything about Good or Evil. That kind of judgment is beyond my ken. But I *am* sayin' that when it starts feelin' as though something's just plain *wrong*, you can usually look to the Source for a clue as to the what and the why of it. It's my job to feel it first, before it gets out of hand and ripples out into the rest of the world. My job and others like me to see what's wrong and nip it in the bud, if'n we can."

"By keeping open eyes and an open mind?" Sara felt a puzzle piece slip into place.

"Yes! Exactly. You have to keep all your talents sharp to catch things early, and the best way to do that is to live here, close to where it all comes from."

Granny sighed, leaned back, and resumed her rocking. "Havin' gifts means havin' the responsibility to use them well. That's why I'm here. That's what my life's all about."

"But Mama didn't stay here, Gran. Why'd she leave if she wasn't supposed to?"

"Well," Granny sighed, "she weren't near as gifted as you or me, Sara-Jean, so I 'spect she didn't feel the weight of it so strongly as I did at her age. Still, she knew what she was leavin' behind. I think she's felt kind of guilty all her life, and that's why she didn't put up too much of a squabble when I asked her to send you to me."

"So you lived here all your life," Sara murmured again, looking out at the eerie glow, listening to the faint, watery noises of secretive swamp things that ventured out only when the sun was gone. After a moment she turned a thoughtful gaze on her grandmother, seeing her in a new kind of light, too; seeing her as someone deeply dedicated rather than merely eccentric.

"Doesn't it get lonely? *Are* you lonely, Granny?"

"Heavens, no, child!" Granny answered with an easy chuckle. "My word! I'm not the only one. Over time, you meet others and you can call on them at need. It's just we're few and far between, so it's like havin' neighbors a right long ways off." She continued in a confiding tone, "Guardin' the Source has its rewards, too, you know. The more in touch with it you are, the more it seems like it knows when you have a powerful want or need, and it kind of keeps *you* balanced in return by sendin' you what's necessary. That's a real simple way to tell it, but that's how I met your grandpa."

Sara had never known her mother's father, and had wondered about what he was like from time to time. So she jumped at the opportunity Granny seemed to be offering.

"Tell me about Granddad. How'd you meet him when you were all alone way out here?"

A warm smile creased Granny's weathered face and a spark of mischief glinted in her eyes. "I'm after thinkin' the Source sent him to me. That's the only way I can figure such a meetin' as we had. Your grandpa were a professor, a studier of plants and bug life. One day he said the swamp just called him and he couldn't say no. He found his way out here and capsized right up against this here front yard.

"After I pulled him out of the mud and cleaned him up, we got to talkin'. Turns out we had a lot in common. We both felt somethin' special in the bayou. I helped him explore far and away to places he would never otherwise have seen. Days turned into weeks and we ended up gettin' hitched on the shore by Chalmette.

"We were together a right long time." Granny's voice trailed off, visions of past love and light flitting once more before her mind's eye.

"What happened to him, Gran?" Sara had always thought it would have been nice to have two full, matched sets of grandparents, even if one set stayed in a swamp and didn't visit. Like nice, solid bookends to one's genealogy.

"Well, that's a long story, child. In the end, the swamp took him. I said that Good and Evil are beyond my ken, but I think I can pass judgment on the ones who I 'spect had a hand in your grandpa's bein' led astray and lost. I'd say they're pure Evil through and through. But I do still try to keep an open mind on it. They're part of the Source's balance, same as me," she ended in a grudging tone.

"So bad things are out here, too, trying to *un*balance the Source?" Sara found this disturbing at best, alarming at worst.

"Yes, indeed. Yes, indeed." Granny saw Sara's look of consternation. "Think on it, child. Look at the swamp all picked out in green fire. Would you know that light was somethin' special if'n you hadn't seen the bayou without it? No! You'd just take it for granted. Balance is the same way. No one side can push things too far without upsettin' the whole boat. Bad as I feel about the other side, I have to take the view that they're necessary, too. I don't like it, but the Source and its upkeep are beyond the likes and dislikes of one old woman."

Granny hitched her shoulders back and stretched her neck as though trying to work a kink out of it. "I think that's about enough for today, girl. You've taken in more than I intended and I'm feelin' kind of puny after all that hikin' about. I'm for bed now."

Sara turned from looking into the pearl-lit foliage surrounding the cabin. "Granny?"

"Oh, land sake's. One more. What is it, child?" Granny sighed, resigned to yet another question and a possibly lengthy explanation.

"Can I go for a walk out there? Right now? Alone?"

Granny tilted her head, peering deep into the marshy night. "Well, I 'spect it's safe enough, just so's you don't go too far. You remember the cautions I gave you every day when you first came to me?"

"Sure I do."

"Snakes and 'gators and bugs and bogs!" they chanted in a singsong rhythm. "Snakes and 'gators and bugs and bogs!"

Granny smiled at the childish recitation. "All right. Since you can see the swamp-light now, I guess you can take a short walk."

Privately, she was doubly relieved. There would be no more discussion that evening, so she could seek her bed in peace. More importantly, Sara was taking time to think things over, which meant she hadn't been put off by the sudden strangeness, jumping to the conclusion that city life would suit her better. In addition, she was venturing out into the swamp alone, which meant she already felt a kinship and safety within it.

All in all, not a bad day's accomplishments, Granny told herself a short while later as she pulled a twig-comb through her hair and readied herself for a good, deep sleep.

6

SARA STOOD UP, dusted off the seat of her jeans, and jumped from the porch steps to a dry, rushy spot with cattails that looked like soft, green puffs in the swamp's night-glow. She made her way with care, but also with confidence, reveling in her new ability to traverse the darkened landscape.

Despite her assurance that she wouldn't go far, Sara found herself drawn deeper and deeper into the bayou. The peaceful quiet of natural sounds and the gentle illumination worked as a salve to her churning, confused thoughts. She was in a peculiar state of amazement to have discovered there was something unique and extraordinary about herself. She sniffed when she thought of Amy-Dean and Michael living their normal, predictable lives back home. How good it would feel to have them realize that their little sister, Sara-Jean, wasn't just a pest and a bother! She could hardly wait to rub their noses in her new-found talents.

The idea brought her up short. The only way her talents would have any relevance, any worth, would be if she did indeed elect to stay in the swamp and, as Granny said, learn the swamp-works. And that would mean leaving her old life behind. Leaving her parents, her siblings, her friends, her school. She didn't suppose it would happen all at once, but in the end she would be carrying on the same solitary life as her grandmother, great-grandmother, great-great-grandmother, and who knew how many more greats, reaching how far back. A creeping sensation of being watched by rank upon rank of ghostly women draped in mossy rags sent a shudder rippling up Sara's spine. She halted, taking a good, long look over each shoulder until she was sure she was still alone.

She blew her breath out in a puff, watched it fog up in the cool night air, and shook her head. It was just too much to consider right now. There was comfort in knowing she had a few days left before they'd row back to where Mama would be waiting to take her home to her safe, comfortable life. *Boring life*, a corner of her mind whispered in rebellion. *Well, everything won't be decided tonight*, she told herself. *Might as well enjoy getting to see the swamp all strange and aglow.*

She stopped her cautious path-picking and looked around. Although the faint luminescence surrounded her, it looked as though there was an uncommonly bright concentration of light a short way off to her left. Moving with a quiet and a care that befitted the night, Sara walked until she reached what turned out to be a little grotto-like glade she'd never encountered, or at least never noticed, in the daylight.

For several moments she remained still and silent, drinking in the beauty of the place. Although brighter than the surrounding swamp, the light wasn't harsh. It was soft and pearly as though a ghost or an angel had breathed all over it. A vagrant breeze stirred lacy ferns, drawing Sara's eyes lower. The puddles and springs that were murky brown by day now contained small, sparkling lights that added a golden-amber color to their depths. Sara thought it looked as though tiny fairy candles had been lit far below the surface, like a gathering of magic, a celebration of strange.

As odd as it all seemed, she moved closer until she was right at the edge of the little glade. She found a seat on an old, water-logged stump and wondered why the beauty of this place touched her heart in ways different from anything she'd ever seen before. It caught in her throat and threatened to send a tear tracking down her cheek, but she managed to gulp it back before it escaped. She wondered how she would ever tell her mother or father, or Amy-Dean or Michael, about how enchantingly lovely a swamp could be after sunset. No one would understand. No one would believe her. She sniffled, a small surrender to self-pity.

"I wish I had someone to share this with right now," Sara whispered.

Somehow speaking or moving seemed unwelcome in this place. So she sat, letting the hush surround her, letting her gaze wander as the slight movements of wind and water revealed delicate variations in shades of green, gold, and amber. For the first time since she'd seen the laputa birds, Sara felt completely relaxed and peaceful. Leaning back against a tree trunk abutting her stump, she bent one leg and clasped her hands around her knee. She took a deep breath and felt something tense loosen in her chest, as though it had been coiled all her life just waiting for release.

"Bubble-SPLASH! Bubble-SPLASH!" a high-pitched, piercing voice shrieked.

Sara froze. Despite her relaxed posture, her heart tripped into overtime and her mouth went dry. A tiny corner of her mind congratulated her on keeping still instead of crying out in alarm. One of Granny's first instructions when Sara was seven had been, "Until you know what you're dealin' with, don't move. Might be you just attract somethin' to you that otherwise would have gone on its sweet way without even noticin' you were nigh."

"Bubble-SPLASH! Bubble-SPLASH!"

Sara held her position, trying to get her suddenly laboring lungs under control and glancing all about the glade. Her gaze caught and fastened on movement. A tiny, silvery ball traced a graceful arc from the tangled foliage at the top of a cypress tree into the water pooled around its roots. As the ball disappeared below the surface, the water's phosphorescence spurted up and then settled in a luminous froth before going back to glassy smoothness.

"Bubble-SPLASH!" giggled the chirping voice that Sara realized was also coming from the swaying uppermost branches of the leaning cypress. Moving only her eyes, she squinted as she tried to see what had intruded on her peaceful reverie. Despite the creature's joyful sound, she wasn't yet sure if it posed a threat. After much frowning and peering, she saw it.

Sara thought she had never beheld anything so strangely wild convey such a sense of elegance. Perched near the cypress' trunk was something with smooth, pale, gray skin. She could see its large, dark eyes and long, shiny, gray-green hair. It was scantily clothed in what she guessed to be woven strings of moss. Lined up on the branch beside it were a row of spheres like the silvery one that had arced its way into the water. As she strained to see more, the little creature, which couldn't have been more than eight inches tall, picked up another ball with its long, slender fingers. Demonstrating grace worthy of a ballerina, it held the ball high, twirled several times on the mossy tree limb, and pitched the silvery orb into the night air. As the ball traced a faintly glittering path down to the water, the little creature's wild giggle rang like chimes.

Clapping its delicate hands together, it cried out once again, "Bubble-SPLASH! Bubble-SPLASH!"

Sara didn't think it looked dangerous. It was enchanting; almost fairy-like, but with an organic kind of swamp twist to it. Still, appearances could be deceiving, so she thought she'd try for a closer look before making her presence known. She was beginning to feel a little awkward as she continued to strain to see the thing out of the corner of her eye. She turned her head the merest fragment of a degree.

You would think she had screamed aloud, or fired a cannon, or brandished a flaming torch. The tiny creature whirled with eldritch speed to face the intruder. Sara saw delicately formed, grayish lips purse in a surprised, "O." Before she could move again or make a sound, the wraith-like little thing had whisked behind the cypress' trunk. In her peripheral vision, Sara thought she saw other movements. They were so quick and widespread that she had the momentary impression of no real movement at all, but rather of the entire landscape *shifting*.

She'd obviously been seen, so she didn't think there was any benefit to be had in remaining frozen. Sara stood up, scanning the glade for anything that would give a clue as to where or what the elfin creature was.

Nothing.

After a few more minutes of sheer concentration and focus, she decided there would be no encore. At least not tonight. She took a few steps closer to the leaning cypress upon which the creature had perched and bent over the pool at its feet. Aided by the pearly-green glow of the glade, she found one of the silvery balls the creature had been pitching into the water. She fished it out, and realized it was formed from crumpled up leaves that were covered with a pale, platinum fuzz. Several others were scattered nearby. It seemed they'd been knocked off the tree limb in the creature's haste to hide itself.

Sara gathered up the little spheres. With painstaking care, she arranged them in a pyramid at the base of the cypress.

"I'm sorry!" she called up into the treetops. "I didn't mean to scare you!"

When there was no response, she resigned herself to the journey back to the cabin. At the edge of the glade she turned one last time.

"I put your leaf-balls by the tree. Again, I'm sorry I frightened you!"

Sara stepped out into the less-brightly lit area beyond the glade. Followed by a silence that felt more brooding and watchful than before, she made her way home.

7

SARA WOULD HAVE loved to shake Granny awake and find out what she could tell her about her adventure, her first solo trip into the bayou night, but Granny was asleep, a muffled snore acting like a "keep out" sign. Sara recalled her grandmother mentioning feeling puny after the day's hike and thought better of disturbing her. She prepared herself for bed with as little noise as possible.

It was a long time before she dozed off herself. When she did finally fall asleep, unsettling dreams of glowing fairies tossing pale lozenges off of cliffs as a frantic Sara ran about trying to catch them, calling, "They're souls! Stop it! They're souls!" prevented her from getting any real rest. Granny had to call her several times in the morning before the aroma of fresh griddle cakes penetrated her sleep-fogged mind and reminded her she was safe indoors and another day had dawned on the bayou.

"Long night?" Granny queried, amusement tweaking the corners of her mouth upward.

"Ummmmm," Sara grunted with a distinct lack of grace as she sat up, lowered her feet to the wood plank floor, and rubbed her eyes with the heels of both hands.

"First time out in the night, it's easy to get bewitched by every little thing," Granny clucked. "What time did you get back, girl?"

Sara was surprised to find that she *did* have an idea of the time, considering there were no clocks in the cabin, Granny didn't wear a watch, and she always left her own at home for fear she'd lose or break it, if she brought it with her to the swamp. In fact, the only time-telling device she'd ever seen on her visits was an old bronze sundial nailed down to a wide, flat stump in a clearing just to the south of the cabin. Its patina of verdigris gave it an ancient appearance. The coloring also served to camouflage it from casual observation. Sara had discovered it quite by accident on her first visit when she had needed someplace to sit while she tried to scrape muck from her sneakers—the result of a small mishap with a well-disguised boggy spot.

"A little after midnight, I guess." Sara yawned. "But I saw the strangest thing while I was out there." She related her encounter with the tiny denizen of the cypress and the "bubble-splash" game it had been playing.

"My word!" Granny exclaimed as she plopped down on one of the kitchen chairs. "You're progressin' right fast, my girl, but even if you were an old hand and had lived here for nigh on seventy years, like me, you saw yourself a rare thing indeed." Sara was beginning to feel little bursts of pride in her own abilities each time her grandmother remarked on her precociousness. Nevertheless, she had to admit to herself this pride shared almost equal space with a nervous wariness about where it all could lead.

"I'm thinkin' you saw yourself a swamp-jenny," Granny continued.

"Its name is Jenny?" Sara wished she'd known; it might have made a difference if the creature had heard her call it by name.

"No, child. That's not its name. That's what it *is*."

"Huh?" This was the only response Sara's still sleep-addled brain could produce.

"A swamp-jenny. No one knows if they even *have* names. They pretty much keep to themselves and avoid bein' seen by the likes of us." Granny tilted her head in consideration. "Are you sure there was only the one? This time of year they usually travel in groups or at least pairs. If you saw a jenny, there was probably a swamp-jack not far away." She shook her head in consternation. "They breed like rabbits, they do."

Sara remembered the odd sensation of a panoramic shift that she'd seen out of the corners of her eyes. She told her grandmother about it.

"Yep. Yep. I bet'cha there were others lurkin' about in all the treetops. That glade sounds like the kind of place they'd favor. That's a rare thing indeed. A *very* rare thing . . ." she trailed off as she finished setting syrup and butter out on the kitchen table.

Sara washed and dressed and took her place across from Granny.

"Let me pass on to you what I know, or at least have heard tell about the swamp-jennies and swamp-jacks, girl," Granny said, still marveling at Sara's encounter. "As near as anyone can discover (and that means generations of livin' at close quarters with them, even if you can't see them), they kind of share a mind among them."

Sara gave her a skeptical look.

Granny chewed and swallowed. "Either they live all throughout the swamp, or there's one great, big community of them that moves mighty fast from one end t' the other.

"Legend has it they know everything that goes on around here, and even as far into the bayou as the Source itself. You might say that if the Source is this place's Power, then the swamp-jennies and swamp-jacks are its Spirit. It'd be a wonderful thing indeed to make acquaintance with the likes of them."

"Why's that?" Sara asked around a mouthful of griddle cake. "This one seemed cute, and I'd love to see more of them, but it also looked kind of silly. What use are they?"

"Land sakes, child. Those little swamp-folk could be like a news network if they took a likin' to you." Granny leaned forward, elbows on the table, as she considered the possible benefits of making friends with the swamp-sprites.

"Say an unwelcome visitor is comin' your way. Why, a jenny or jack could warn you. I 'spect, if they *really* liked you, they could even lead that visitor astray and save you the trouble of an unpleasant encounter. Or maybe they could tell you, in their own way, of course, about things that are goin' on in the swamp. Maybe warn you *before* you start feelin' that thing's are gettin' out of balance." Granny's eyes looked dream-filled, as though they were focused on something far away.

"I bet if I'd had a swamp-sprite on my side your grandpa would still be here," she said in a hushed voice. "Or at least I'd know for sure what part was played by those two evil, twisted, sick . . ." she caught herself with a jolt. "Sorry, Sara-Jean. Even after twenty years I still wouldn't say 'no' to gettin' some revenge for my Cal being taken from me." She gave a gusty sigh and poured herself another cup of chicory bark tea.

"But I'm gettin' off the track. I hear tell that the swamp-jennies and jacks are kinda like the Source in they don't tell right from wrong, or good from bad the way we do."

Sara finished sopping up her last bit of syrup and gave Granny a puzzled look. "What do you mean by that, Gran? How could you trust them if they don't know the difference?"

"Well, this is all hearsay, mind you, but they're powerful playful creatures. Why, it sounds like even that one you saw was playin' a game. They're supposed to like shiny, pretty things and such. There's an old story about a swamp-jack that led a man travelin' the bayou right into a bog. The whole time he was a-strugglin' to free his self, that little jack was laughin' and laughin'. It wasn't until the last moment when the man went under the mud that the jack realized something final-like might come of its joke. It dangled a vine down to his last, graspin' hand, and he was able to pull himself out. When he finally got home, he told his kin that he got the feelin' that the swamp-jack only saved him because it didn't want to lose a plaything that amused it so much."

Sara shook her head in consternation. "That doesn't sound like a creature whose company I'd value. Seems kind of cruel."

Granny began clearing dishes. "The point is the swamp-jack didn't mean any ill. It just wanted to have fun. I think that's what makes them dangerous—that they don't operate on the same set of values or limitations humans do. But I don't think there's any true bad in them. Just playfulness misdirected, maybe." She murmured to herself, "I bet you just have to be mindful of how they see things. I bet . . ."

Granny dumped the breakfast dishes into the large, soap-filled washing bucket. She straightened, pushing both hands into the small of her back as she groaned. "Land sakes, girl. I'm still feelin' kinda washed-out after yesterday. Maybe I need a tonic. What do you say we take it easy today and go collect some lemon-weed? I've got a powerful hankerin' for some and it's a pleasant walk to where they grow."

The thought of a simple outing without any more strange revelations appealed to Sara. She'd like the time to think over all that had happened on this eventful summer visit. Also, Granny did look a trifle under the weather. A peaceful stroll might do her good.

"Will we be gone long? Should I pack us a lunch?" Sara remembered how hungry she'd grown during yesterday's hike.

"Not a bad idea, child," her grandmother agreed. "There's some bread, cheese, and smoked ham in the larder. While I get my walkabout clothes on, you could make us a couple of sandwiches."

As Granny was getting ready, Sara made their lunch and filled the antique bottle they'd used yesterday with fresh drinking water. As she tried to do a neat job of packing everything into the rubberized pouch Granny had used before, she noticed a roll of tinfoil sitting on a shelf in the larder cupboard.

"Granny? Do you think we'll be going anywhere near that glade where the swamp-jenny was?" she called over her shoulder.

"Oh, I wouldn't count on findin' that place again. Leastways, not in the daytime. I'm amazed you wandered into it and saw a jenny at all. It'd be a wonder indeed if'n you ran into another so soon . . . or *ever.*"

Recalling Granny having mentioned how the swamp-jennies and swamp-jacks were enamored of shiny playthings, Sara tore off a length of foil and crumpled it into three lumpy balls. She put them in her jacket pocket, telling herself that *nothing* that had happened during the last few days was ordinary, so it wouldn't hurt to be prepared in case the pattern continued. Besides, she still felt a little guilty about scaring the swamp-jenny. Maybe she could smooth things over with a bribe of shiny, foil balls. From what she'd just been told, it might be a good idea to try to get on the little creature's good side, even if the human value of "good" didn't apply in swamp-sprite world.

δ

WHEN GRANNY EMERGED onto the front porch, Sara was ready for a fine day's outing. She'd tied the pouch containing their picnic lunch to her belt in imitation of how she'd seen her grandmother do it the day before.

Granny smiled to see Sara copy her, but reminded herself that this was no guarantee that the girl would elect to copy her entire lifestyle and take up permanent residence in the bayou. The choice was still pending.

Sara was gratified to see they were setting out in the same direction she remembered taking the night before. She didn't know if she'd recognize the place without its enchanted phosphorescent appearance, but she kept an eager eye out for a leaning cypress.

Unfortunately, there were quite a few trees that fit that description.

Nonetheless, as they trudged on in companionable silence, Sara thought she saw what she was looking for.

"Gran, wait." She saw a murky pool of water at the base of a familiar looking tree with a large, flat stump not far away. "Gran! I think this is the place."

Granny stopped and scanned the treetops. "Even if it is, girl, you won't find that swamp-jenny still here. They're even scarcer in the daylight hours than they are in the dark." With that, she resumed her steady pace toward the patch of lemon-weed she'd picked as their destination for the day.

Sara couldn't help but feel a little disappointed. Then, remembering the foil balls in her pocket, she made a quick detour to the base of the cypress. There, nestled on the damp ground among the tree's roots was a crumpled, fuzzy gray leaf. Disappointment was replaced by a delighted grin as she recalled the leafy, little spheres she'd stacked at the base of the tree when she'd apologized to the jenny. With no time to waste, she scooped the lumps of tinfoil from her pocket and placed them in a prominent position on a low branch, hoping that nothing disturbed them until a swamp-jenny or swamp-jack found them.

Mission accomplished, she hurried to catch up with her grandmother.

The sun was at its zenith and half the day was gone. Granny stopped and heaved a weary sigh of satisfaction. "Here we are, girl. Finest crop of lemon-weed you're likely to find this side of heaven."

Privately, never having given much consideration to lemon-weed before, Sara didn't think she was likely to go in search of any no matter *what* side of heaven she found herself on.

Granny's breathing was a little heavy, and she looked a bit ashen, so Sara suggested they eat before harvesting any of the pale yellow grasses surrounding them. As they sat among the twisted limbs of a tortured-looking oak, Granny regaled her with generations of swamp-lore pertaining to lemon-weed.

Sara learned that it could be dried and pounded into powder that drew infection out of a wound when used as a poultice. It could be nibbled raw to freshen one's breath and help slake thirst (although Sara didn't think thirst would ever be a problem when so much water was part and parcel of the landscape). And lemon-weed could be brewed into a tea, which was what Granny aimed to do for her "tonic." Then her grandmother extended her lecture, waxing expansive on subjects merely lemon-weed-related.

"Do you recall what the *opposite* of this here lemon-weed is, girl?" Granny queried, a glint of expectation in her eye.

Momentarily taken aback by the sudden question, Sara blinked, feeling the way she did in class when her teacher, Mrs. Caruthers, took her by surprise with crafty questions meant to gage whether or not she'd been woolgathering.

"C'mon, child! You know this. It's not yellow. It's . . ." Granny drew out her hint, a tiny bit of impatience edging her voice.

"Blue!" Sara exclaimed as sketchy memories of the information imparted of an evening on the porch steps swam their way up from the depths of her first year's visit, when she had worked more on presenting a sullen exterior than paying attention to her grandmother's tales.

"That's right," Granny coaxed. "It's blue. And lemon-weed looks warm, but this is . . . ?"

"Cold!" Sara dredged up more than she thought she could. "Cold-burr. It's cold-burr; that blue powdery-looking seed pod you showed me that grows on a prickly shrub."

"Excellent!" Granny was gratified to learn that Sara hadn't managed to block out everything she'd tried to teach her while in the depths of juvenile rebellion.

"And . . . and it's used for just the opposite of lemon-weed," Sara continued, feeling triumphant. "Cold-burr can be ground up, burned for its fumes, or put into food or drink, and used to calm you down or even put you to sleep if you're having a restless night." Pleased at her own performance, Sara smiled and brushed a vagrant insect away from her perspiring brow. "I could have used some of that last night." She sighed.

"Why's that, girl?"

So she told Granny about her dream of the souls being pitched over a cliff by a version of a swamp-jenny that was much more wicked than the one she'd actually seen.

"Hmmmm . . ."

The cautious hum was Granny's only response, but she seemed to be giving the dream more consideration than Sara thought it merited. It was just a muddled-up version of the things she'd encountered in the swamp so far, although she was surprised that she could still recall it in such detail. Usually, if she remembered a dream at all, it faded rather quickly, dispersing like a puff of smoke by mid-morning.

Sara was getting a little overwhelmed with the wonders of lemon-weed and its brethren. They had finished their sandwiches and the sun was shining at an angle that made the patch of weed before them look enticingly golden. The warmth of the day caused a faint, citrus fragrance to hover over the entire area. Sara thought her grandmother looked a trifle better for the rest, so she stood up, dusted off her jeans and said, "So, Gran! How do we pick this stuff anyway?"

"Gran! Oh, Gran! G-G-G-Gran! Tell me, Gran! Oh, teach me, G-G-G-Gran!" a sneering, derisive voice called from off to one side and slightly above them.

Shocked, Sara snapped her head around to face the unexpected intrusion as she stepped backward into a puddle, feeling clammy liquid soak its way past her ankles. For a moment she forgot to step back out onto dry land as she saw the source of the ridicule crouched on the trunk of a fallen tree.

The man was so begrimed that Sara couldn't tell how old he was, but judging by the boneless, flexible way he was hunched over, dangling long, thin arms between his knees past a bulbous belly, she estimated him to be younger than her grandmother. Tiny, squinting eyes and a long, drooping nose that resembled a limp pickle rode above a mouth whose downturned corners spoke of a malicious, sour disposition. He was wearing a broken, bent stovepipe hat that failed to disguise long ears with tips so sagging they nearly touched the sparse tufts of hair growing out of them. A shirt with wide red and white stripes was incongruously cheerful despite several rips and stains that looked as though they matched the thin trail of brown tobacco juice tracing a path from the corner of his mouth down one side of his jaw. Brown, patched pants held up by fraying suspenders and oversized work boots, one of which had a sole flapping loose, completed the tawdry portrait of a thoroughly unpleasant character whose acquaintance Sara had no desire to pursue.

Standing on the limb behind him, with one hand on the trunk to help her keep her balance, was a woman who looked like a perfect match for her sneering companion. She glared at Sara and Granny from behind a greasy curtain of tangled hair, a lock of which she continually twisted and untwisted around one finger. A rank-looking piece of burlap belted with a dirty length of twine was her chief clothing. Bony legs dotted with scabs and scratches led down to muddy feet and gnarled, cracked toenails of an unhealthy gray color. Although she hadn't spoken, hostility draped her like a second garment.

Granny gasped as the man cocked his head on its spindly neck to take a closer look at her.

"So, Abra-Lynn, is this the new blood you've been keepin' secret from us all these years? Hmmmm?"

Sara rarely ever heard Granny's given name. Hearing it come from this unsavory creature set her teeth on edge.

"None of your business, Saylish!" Granny snapped.

"Why, is that any way to speak to folks who've come a right long way jes' to pay their respects?" the man continued, obviously enjoying this confrontation. "Malora and I jes' had to meet the newcomer is all. But I got to say from the looks of it, Abra-Lynn, that this 'un won't last more'n a season once *you're* gone."

"Leave her be, Saylish," Granny responded. "She's nothing to do with you."

"No? No, I 'spose not. No more'n Cal was anythin' to do with us!" A bout of uproarious laughter claimed Saylish and Malora, ringing out all the wilder at Granny's stricken expression.

Sara recalled her grandmother's suspicions about Grandpa Cal's disappearance.

"Gran?" Sara was getting angry and a little frightened, too.

"G-G-G-Gran? G-G-G-Gran?" mimicked Saylish. Malora was doubled over, still giggling too hard to do more than chime in with a breathy "G-G-G-" every now and then.

Granny maintained a grim silence, and Sara followed suit, stepping closer to her to present a more solid, unified front against what felt like a threat. For despite being merely a verbal exchange, Sara most definitely felt threatened. It reminded her of back home when the city's school districts had been redefined halfway through the year, forcing her to switch schools at mid-term. She'd been miserable for the first few weeks when a clique of snobby, rich girls had decided to make her the brunt of their bullying. Sara had managed to find her own friends after a while, which seemed to take the fun out of teasing her and sent the mean girls in search of new quarry. Still, Sara never forgot the helpless anguish she'd felt in the face of their cruel sport.

Somehow this teasing seemed much more serious, like the tip of an enormously ancient and ugly iceberg composed of frozen grudges.

After a few moments of one-sided hilarity, the grimy couple wheezed to a stop, wiping tears of merriment from their eyes.

"Oh, Abra-Lynn, we didn't come here to dredge up ol' history," Saylish confided in an oily voice that nevertheless sounded on the verge of a perpetual whine. "No, indeedy! We came here to tell you 'bout *our* new family member. Seein' as you got one of your own here, I 'spect you'll be right glad for us."

Granny hadn't moved from her seat amid the oak limbs where they'd had their lunch. Her unblinking eyes glared at the visitors, her only movement a twitching muscle as her jaw clenched and unclenched in fury. Sara glanced at her grandmother and thought she'd never seen such a look of pure disgust, even loathing, on anyone's face, let alone that of calm, affable Granny.

Saylish twisted about to look at Malora, who was muffling the last of her giggling fit behind the soiled edge of her coarsely woven neckline.

"Malora, my sweet," he cooed, "fetch our new addition so's we can introduce him proper to Abra-Lynn and the runty, li'l newcomer."

With a look that Sara could only describe as evil glee, the woman leaned around the bole of the tree trunk and grasped something with both hands. "C'mon you stupid, li'l filth," she snarled.

Grunting with effort, she dragged an amorphous, pinkish blob onto the branch where she stood. Sara watched in horror as Malora administered an unceremonious kick to the thing. With a sound like a half-filled soccer ball bladder being punched, the rosy pink mass fell to the ground at Saylish's feet. With a sluggish, gelatinous, rolling motion that spoke of pain, it twisted around until two large, soft, dark pools turned their mournful regard on Granny and Sara.

Granny let out a shuddering breath and rose to her feet, shaking. "Noooooo . . . !" It was more moan than exclamation.

The blood retreated from Granny's face, leaving her skin the color of parchment. Sara had never seen her look so frail.

A wave of unreasoning fear washed over Sara. Something was horribly wrong, but she didn't know what. Clearly, this was more than just the disgust engendered by the presence of Saylish and Malora; more than a demonstration of cruelty to another living creature.

Saylish gave a loud bellow of laughter at Granny's reaction. "I thought you'd like it, Abra-Lynn. I told Malora that we couldn't waste another day w'thout bringin' our pride 'n' joy to say howdy-doo-doo-doo." The words were crowed with triumph.

Complexion shock-white, Granny stared at the quivering, pink mass, unable to look away from the endless sorrow swimming in its eyes.

"Nothin' to say, old woman?" Malora spat out like venom.

"This here's our adopted *son*, Abra-Lynn. Say hello to *Froggy*!" Saylish delivered another vicious kick to the helpless, cringing creature at his feet, sending both him and Malora into fresh gales of cackling laughter.

Granny swayed, but remained upright. Sara stood ready to support her should it become necessary, but she didn't want to step in just yet and risk making her grandmother look weak to the repulsive pair before them. It felt important to look strong and as invulnerable as possible.

"Well, we oughta be on our way," Saylish gasped as this latest wave of mirth ebbed. "We jes' wanted to let you know our family's growin', same as yours, Abra-Lynn. C'mon, Malora, we got work to do if'n we wanna make sure Froggy's not an only child." Chuckling to himself with wicked pleasure, Saylish jumped back over the tree limb on which he'd been crouching and slogged off, flapping his loose boot sole every other step.

Malora lowered herself down to the ground next to the helpless pink blob and kicked it along before her as she followed in Saylish's wake. Sara could hear her muttering curses as she toed Froggy, switching feet every few steps to keep their progress on track.

The trio had disappeared and the natural sounds of the swamp held sway once again. Granny felt behind her for her seat among the oak limbs and collapsed with a small cry of such dreadful grief that Sara fell to her knees beside her, searching the beloved, old face even as anxious lines etched her own brow.

"Gran, what's wrong? Are you alright? Who were those . . . people? What was that thing they called their son?" She had quite forgotten Granny's dislike of being peppered with a whole bevy of questions at once. But Granny didn't seem to have the strength or mind to care at the moment.

"That was Saylish and Malora Muckle," she responded in a faint, shocked voice. "And that thing they called Froggy was . . . it was . . . oh, Sara-Jean, remember what I showed you flowing to the Source yesterday?"

Sara nodded, a vision of the pastel lozenges floating in tranquility clear in her mind's eye. A sick, unnamed dread welled up in her stomach, feeling like an innate omen impossible to name or ignore.

"Froggy's a *soul*, child. They've trapped . . . they've *enslaved* a *soul*!"

To Sara's horror, Granny covered her face with both hands and wept in great, gulping, disconsolate sobs.

9

HER GRANDMOTHER SEEMED to recover somewhat from their encounter with the Muckles, and Sara knew they should return home without delay. Granny didn't argue. She still looked sickly and was uncharacteristically passive. Sara grabbed a few handfuls of the lemon-weed they'd come to harvest and stowed it in the now empty lunch pouch.

Sara led the way home, unmindful of how she instinctively knew the path back to the cabin. She settled Granny in her rocking chair with a blanket tucked around her. She pulled the lemon-weed from the pouch, rinsed it off and, without asking directions, chopped it into fine bits, and put it in Granny's old earthenware teapot. Having filled the pot with water and placed it on a steel grid over the flames she'd coaxed back to life in the fireplace, she left what she hoped would be an effective tonic to brew and went out on the porch to check on her grandmother.

Sara was reassured to see Granny looking a little better, if still ashy and fretful over the day's events.

"How are you feeling, Gran?" she asked in a gentle, sick-room tone. "I'm not sure if I did it right, but I've got some lemon-weed tea brewing."

"Why, thank you, child." Granny roused herself from staring into the trees, gaze blank with worry. She sat up a little straighter and turned to Sara with a grave expression. "I'm sorry, Sara-Jean. I didn't think anything like this would happen. Especially not so soon after your seein' the laputa and just beginnin' to come into your birthright, so to speak. Land sakes, you haven't even had time to choose your path yet." Her weak murmur was filled with regret.

Sara ignored the twisting that happened in her stomach every time the apparently inevitable choice was mentioned. Right now it seemed more important to find out what the encounter with the Muckles and their alleged "son" meant and why it was having such a tremendously troubling effect on her grandmother.

She took a deep breath as she sorted out where to begin. Before Sara could think her way through the day's troubles and decide on an opening question, Granny spoke.

"Those two we ran into today, well, you might have guessed on your own by now that I 'spect they had somethin' to do with your grandfather . . . my Cal . . . disappearin'," Granny said.

Sara kept silent and sat very still.

"That's why I didn't want them gettin' to know too much about you. It's bad enough they know I got me a possible apprentice without their knowin' just how much you can already see. If 'n they knew how powerful the blood is runnin' in you, Sara-Jean, they might take a notion to speed you on your way to the same fate I'm bettin' they fixed up for my Cal."

A shiver shuddered its way through Sara's entire body. "Why would they do something like that?" Why would someone who didn't even know her want to harm her? Privately, she didn't think she was important enough for anyone to go to that kind of trouble, but that might just be the result of having heard her sister, Amy-Dean, voice the same opinion with big-sister frequency. "Exactly who were those people?"

"Those were the Muckles. Saylish and Malora." Granny heaved a deep sigh that spoke of a long-suffering acquaintance. "Remember how I told you about balance, 'specially the Source's balance?"

Sara nodded.

"Things that unbalance the Source can be of the natural variety, like pollution or any big upheaval in the land. That kind of thing is what I, and those like me, deal with most. We just sense it before it gets too far and then find ways to counteract whatever's throwin' things out of whack. Don't get me wrong; it's not easy. But so far it's been do-able with a little plannin' and a lot of effort." Granny shifted in her chair, drawing the blanket Sara had brought her a little higher, as though warding off a chill.

"But there's somethin' so much, much worse, child. Just as there are people like us, I mean, *me*," she gave Sara an apologetic little nod which Sara supposed was in deference to her having yet to make the steadily approaching choice. "There are those who work against us, who *un*balance the Source and who take a wicked kind of glee in it when the trouble spills over into the rest of the world."

"The Muckles?" Sara ventured.

Granny gave a definitive nod. "Their usual way of operatin' is to cause some ruckus and strife for us who balance. When my Cal vanished, I was right useless for a month of Sundays, I was. It fell to others to take up the slack." She gave her head a rueful shake and Sara a sheepish look.

"It's a hard lesson I hope you'll be able to avoid for a good, long spell, if not forever. Sometimes you have to put your own sorrows aside and keep pushin' on for the sake of the bigger picture. Anyway, I'm older and I know better now.

"But this, this *abomination* today, why that's a whole different kettle of fish." Granny's posture stiffened and her expression took on an angry (even *fierce*, Sara thought) aspect.

"What those Muckles have done this time. This is worse than all of the nasty tricks and hurts they've inflicted on the likes of us durin' the course of their entire, mal-formed, misbegotten lives." Then a light of comprehension came into her eyes. "Why, I bet that's why I've been feelin' so poorly for the last couple days. And, sensitive as you're turnin' out to be, I'm a-bettin' it's why you had such a dream-troubled sleep last night. We're both feelin' the Source bein' shoved out of balance worse than it's been shoved in a passel of generations."

While Granny muttered heartfelt curses and imprecations against Saylish and Malora, Sara went inside to check on the lemon-weed tea's progress. The steaming, saffron liquid smelled more like freshly sliced tangerines than lemons. The brief exposure she had to it while pouring out a good-sized mug for her grandmother cleared Sara's mind and gave her a boost of energy despite the late hour and the disturbing events of the day.

As she returned to the porch and handed Granny the invigorating brew, her spirits were somewhat lighter. If the Muckles were playing havoc with the Source's balance, then she and her grandmother would simply have to find a way to remedy the situation. So potent was the effect of the tea's vapors, Sara didn't question her new confidence. As Granny sipped her lemon-weed tea, Sara delved deeper into the particulars of the Muckles' latest exploit.

"Why do you think they call that poor thing Froggy? Do you think maybe it's a frog's soul?" she asked. She thought maybe the situation wouldn't be as dire if it was a very small creature's soul at stake.

"Oh, I don't know." Granny sighed, gazing into the depths of her mug of tea. "It doesn't really matter *whose* soul it is. Anything as absolutely, horribly wrong as stoppin' a soul from makin' its rightful journey goes so far against the natural law of things, it makes no difference if it's the soul of a man, a frog, or a gnat. *It's just plain wrong.*"

Sara gathered that in this instance, there were no gray areas. The matter was black and white. She abandoned her hopes that the infraction of soul-entrapment might not be as catastrophic as Granny made it out to be.

She had been keeping a close eye on her grandmother, but now Sara rocked back on her heels and turned her attention to the dark, bayou night, hoping to draw reassurance from the ghostly glow.

The optimism she'd breathed in with the aroma of lemon-weed fled.

"Granny, look! What's happened to the light?" Sara had noticed that as each hour had passed during the previous night, the pale, phosphorescent illumination that limned the landscape had grown a bit brighter, a bit more glittery and, well . . . *magical*. Now, the opposite seemed to be happening. The foliage and pools were duller. The glow was a sickly, livid, almost fleshy color.

"Oh, my dear goodness," Granny breathed. Her grip on the mug of tea loosened, allowing some of the liquid to splash onto the floorboards before she mastered her reaction and righted it. "Oh, Sara-Jean, this is bad. Really bad."

The quiet calm of the statement did more to unsettle Sara than any of the previous shocked exclamations or even the snide jibes and insults thrown by the Muckles. It was like standing on a placid shore, looking at a beautiful sunset while simultaneously noticing a tidal wave speeding toward you, deadly and unstoppable. Sara looked to Granny for clarification.

"When the balance is wrenched this far off course, the things that we can see, that we use as earmarks of the gifts our blood bequeaths us, begin to fade. If things swing all the way over to the Muckles' side, it's said that in the end, we won't be able to see or feel or sense *any* of the Power around us."

Sorrowfully, softly, Granny turned to Sara. "We'll be blind, Sara. We'll be blind, and where will the world be then?"

10

SARA SWALLOWED AGAINST the dryness in her mouth. She'd only just begun to see this strange world her grandmother lived in, but already she was loath to give it up. It wasn't fair. She was supposed to have a choice. The Muckles and their meddling were taking that away from her. Anger began a slow burn deep in her chest. No! This was not the way it would all end. Not for her and not for Granny. She gripped the porch railing, bracing herself with arms stiffly straight.

"What do we have to do, Gran? Just tell me," she asked in a very grim tone.

"Well, first thing is to set that soul, that *Froggy*, back on its rightful course." Granny's voice was fainter than Sara would have liked. She sounded doubtful, or weary beyond endurance.

"The next thing is to make sure Saylish and Malora stop. You recall they mentioned growin' their family?"

Sara nodded, remembering also the shudder of revulsion that had crept over her at the prospect, even though she hadn't been quite sure what that meant.

"We got to find us a way to prevent those two from doin' anything like this ever again. That means we got to figure out how they did it in the first place." Granny pushed herself up out of the rocking chair with visible effort. "But first, before anything else, child, I'll be needin' some rest. Can't rightly see myself trekkin' all the way to the Muckles feelin' like I do."

Disconcerted, Sara watched her grandmother hobble into the cabin.

"What? No, Granny. We have to go now. We can't wait. What if they catch another soul? What if all *this* gets worse?" Sara swept her arm out to encompass the entire landscape and its faded, sickly glow. She swallowed the lump of dread that had formed in her throat. "What if you're right? What if . . . what if we really do go . . . go . . . *blind*?"

Granny's reply drifted out to the porch from where she perched on the edge of her bed. "The Muckles live past the lemon-weed patch toward the east as far again as we hiked today. Too far. Nothin' I can do right now, girl."

Sara's heart wanted to break at the sorrowful tone of resignation.

"Maybe it's age. Maybe it's that nothin' this truly bad has ever pushed the Source so hard; leastwise not in my reckonin'. I'm sorry, Sara-Jean, but you'll just have to wait 'til I get some rest. And then maybe . . . maybe some of the others will get in touch . . . They must be feelin' it, too . . ."

To Sara it sounded like a pronouncement of doom. She watched from the doorway as her grandmother rolled herself into her blanket and dozed off scarcely a minute later, facing the wall, facing away from the night that was no longer lit by a vital, sparkling, pearly green.

Sara turned her back to the cabin's door and gripped the porch railing once more. *No*, she thought. *This can't all be snatched away when it's hardly begun. If I wait for Granny to feel better, it might be too late. I might not be able to see anything but deep darkness by tomorrow night. And if there are others she works with and they're feeling as sickly as she is, then what use would they be . . . ?*

She looked over her shoulder at her Granny engaged in fitful slumber in the large bed redolent of Spanish moss. She wondered when she'd begun to care so deeply for her and for all of this wonderful, strange world to which she'd been introduced. Was it only a couple of days? When she had first set foot on this weathered, old porch, everything had seemed slimy, uncouth, and unbearably boring. Now, just looking into the swamp at night, even with its diminished glow, stirred something deep in her soul. *Like something ancient lifting its head, because its name has finally been called*, Sara mused. The image was so unlike her; another sea-change moving through her spirit, one of poetry and dread and new sensations.

She couldn't lose all this. Not yet.

With light steps, Sara walked back into the cabin's kitchen area and found the water-proofed pouch with its empty antique bottle on the counter where she had left it while preparing the lemon-weed tea. As stealthily as the night, she wrapped some leftover cheese and bread in tinfoil and placed them in the pouch. She uncorked the bottle, but then hesitated, hovering over the barrel of drinking water. After a moment's consideration, she tiptoed to the fireplace, picked up the still steaming teapot, and filled the bottle with the rest of the fragrant, lemony brew.

Standing at the counter, packing the bottle into her pouch, Sara looked up at the tall cupboards reaching to the ceiling where she knew Granny kept dried herbs and other plants endowed with either culinary or medicinal value. Feeling the beginnings of a plan, she opened them and scanned the neatly organized contents. The container of cold-burrs glimmered a faint blue even within the deeply shadowed recesses. She reached as high as she could, grinning with the memory of how Granny had arranged her provisions so that those of questionable merit would defy the reach of seven-year-old Sara's inquisitive fingers. But *eleven*-year-old Sara could tweak the box just enough to bring it closer to the edge of the shelf, where she could tip it over with eleven-year-old dexterity and catch it as it tumbled down.

The box held several fuzzy seed pods still attached to a prickly stem. Something rattled from the box's depths as Sara lifted the pods out, marveling that her fingers felt a slight numbing sensation just from brushing against the dried cold-burrs. Tipping the container to see its contents more fully, she made a small sound of satisfaction when she saw a medium-sized jar filled with shimmering, pale, blue powder. With a careful touch, she fished the jar out and held it up to the light of the one kerosene lantern still burning. The jar was nearly full and was sealed with a layer of paraffin wax topped by a metal screw-top lightly touched with rust. Clearly, the cold-burr powder had been preserved for quite some time, but if the power of the dried pods was any indication, Sara thought the powder in its air-tight jar would be extremely potent.

She wrapped it in an old dish rag and added it to the waterproofed pouch.

She cast a last affectionate look at her grandmother, who was murmuring and fidgeting in her sleep.

"Sorry, Gran. I don't think we can wait for morning," she whispered.

Then Sara was out the door and moving across the treacherous terrain with a grace that would have astonished her, had she seen herself even one week earlier. She looked back at the faint light of the lantern she'd left burning inside the cabin and considered what she was about to do.

Sara at her parents' house would have had to ask permission to walk three blocks to the neighborhood grocery store. Sara at her grandmother's cabin was setting out across miles and miles of unknown, potentially dangerous ground on a rescue mission she couldn't even imagine trying to explain to anyone who wasn't an integral part of the swamp and its haunting strangeness.

And she was setting out alone.

Shaking her head in bemusement at how different things were out here, at how different *she* was, Sara turned her back on Granny's house and melted into the bayou night.

11

THE FIRST FEW hours of Sara's journey weren't too difficult.

Even in the less vibrant illumination of the ailing swamp glow, she was able to recognize that she was on the same path, headed in the same direction that she and Granny had walked earlier on their way to the lemon-weed patch.

A sharp, citrus aroma alerted her when she arrived at the place where Saylish and Malora Muckle had introduced them to poor, tormented Froggy.

Sara stopped, her breathing a little ragged from having pushed herself to travel as quickly as caution and common sense allowed. She found the same tangled roots of the oak tree where they had lunched the previous day and decided it was as good a place as any to rest for a moment and refuel. As she ate the cheese and bread she'd packed, she began to have second thoughts. Looking toward the place where the Muckles had disappeared into the trees and vines sent a thrill of uncertainty through her.

This was Granny's world more than hers. What if something happened to her? Who would find her? Echoes of Granny's words about Granddad Cal and his unknown fate, possibly at the hands of the Muckles themselves, made her mouth go dry. As she tried to swallow the last of her meal, she had to consider the consequences of meeting Saylish and Malora alone in unfamiliar territory. If her grandfather, who had been much more knowledgeable about swamp lore and survival had fallen prey, what was to prevent the same thing from happening to her? Dryness and the sudden rubbery taste of fear had Sara reaching for the bottle of lemon-weed tea with hands that trembled.

Even before tasting it, the fragrance of the brew began to work, dispelling her misgivings. After a good, long draught, she felt her hands steady while her breathing and heartbeat eased. It wasn't the calming effect that cold-burr would have had, she reflected. Rather, it was the aftermath of a dose of unassailable confidence and courage.

"I'll just find the Muckles' place and take a look around," she told herself. "I'll be careful and cautious and no one will see me." She closed the bottle of tea, crumpled up the foil in which her food had been wrapped, and stowed both back in the pouch.

"I'll be fine," she whispered as she hitched the pouch higher on her hip and climbed up the slope to where Saylish and Malora had been hurling taunts at her a few hours ago.

Sara's weariness increased through the long hours of the night. Her eyes strained to find safe passage through the boggy land in the fading, unhelpful swamp glow. At one point she cast about in a thicket of deadfall until she found a reasonably straight tree limb. She used it to test the ground before her as her ability to pick a safe path waned. At first she tried to discern tiny clues that the Muckles had passed the same way. A faint, muddy indentation in the shape of Saylish's ruined boots or Malora's gnarled, bare feet. But the most consistently visible sign was the track of smoothed ground and compressed plant life that spoke of Froggy's tortured passage, booted from side to side as though in some twisted, cruel soccer match.

Every time Sara encountered a brief space in the shallow troughs, her heart constricted with pity as she envisioned the luckless Froggy being kicked viciously enough to render him airborne for a brief space. She gritted her teeth and quickened her steps, telling herself that any discomfort or fear she felt was nothing compared to what Froggy was experiencing.

At long last, only an hour or so before dawn, Sara halted. She wasn't sure at first what had made her stop. It felt like a compulsion to do so. She recalled Granny's admonishments about swamp safety. She held very still, scanning as far as possible from side to side and top to bottom. Then she calmed her own breathing, listening for anything unusual. It hit her within seconds: there were almost no natural noises surrounding her.

Throughout her journey the gentle plops and swishes of nocturnal swamp life had accompanied her like a soft, secretive, background melody. Its sudden absence made her skin crawl. Sara felt unaccountably abandoned. Suppressing an involuntary shudder, she strained her ears . . . and amended her perception that absolute silence reigned.

There *was* a noise! But it didn't sound, well, *natural*.

Somewhere up ahead was a slow, rhythmic *thunk . . . thunk . . . thunk*. It was soft, but persistent. Sara couldn't imagine its source. Nothing she'd encountered in her few years of wandering the bayou around Granny's cabin had ever sounded like that. Convinced that the otherwise silent night was a symptom of surprise at or disapproval of this unidentified noise, she resumed moving forward, but at a slower pace in case whatever was making that noise should prove dangerous.

A dim, crescent moon drifting among sporadic shreds of cloud shone through branches into a clearing directly before her. By now the night glow was little more than a ghost of its previously vibrant, emerald glitter. Sara reflected that it looked more like an infection than the joyous sparkle she had first seen. As the clearing came fully into view, she took refuge behind a scabrous-looking tree trunk. Crouching within the deep shadows at its base, she peered through the gloom and saw she had reached her destination.

To her right, leaning at a precarious angle on semi-rotted pilings, was a structure that made Granny's worn, homey, little shack look like the most wholesome, pristine dwelling ever constructed.

The steep-peaked roof had fallen in on one side. Heavy moss coated the rest of it, except for some ragged holes where an occasional rotted rafter peeped through. Several windows had been cut into the warped walls, but the dim reflection of moonlight showed that only one cracked pane of glass remained among them. A sagging porch with missing floorboards and broken railings completed the picture of neglect. Encroaching plant life and insidious moisture worked against all structures in the bayou, but here they'd been given free reign. Not the slightest attempt was made to minimize their destructive effect.

Sara's lip curled in disgust, recalling how poorly she'd thought of her grandmother's home when she'd first seen it. If something like the Muckles' house had greeted her, she vowed she would have plunged headfirst into the murky, swamp water there and then, and swum her way back to Chalmette. She continued to scan the terrain, taking inventory of the decrepit accumulation of broken objects and trash surrounding the house . . . and . . .

. . . her breath caught.

She stifled an involuntary exclamation.

There, off to one side, was the source of the slow, rhythmic sound that was so out of place in the swamp night.

A crude, wooden pen had been constructed close to the base of one of the rotted pillars that held up a tottering corner of the porch. Four thick beams had been driven into the soggy ground. Four weathered slats that looked as though they'd been pried up from the porch floor were nailed with crooked disregard from beam to beam, approximately four inches above the uneven ground. Within this rustic enclosure was Froggy. As Sara watched, the bruised-looking mass rolled disconsolately from side to side, slapping against first one board of the makeshift pen and then its opposite.

Sara had read a newspaper article once about horses who had been confined to their stalls for over long periods without company or distraction. Out of sheer, desperate boredom some had taken to chewing on their wooden doors and rocking from side to side against their walls. Sara had cried to herself in sympathy for the forlorn animals. Now she felt a similar sorrow well up inside her at the sight and sound of Froggy's hopeless, unthinking movements. She bit her lip to keep from making any noise and peered through the dark at the ramshackle abode she was sure was the official residence of Saylish and Malora Muckle.

Spaces between the boards that formed the house walls were dark, indicating the Muckles were probably still asleep. Sara noted the presence on the porch of a large barrel similar to the one Granny used to hold purified water for drinking and bathing. She also saw the telltale rippling of a slow current passing across a boggy area adjacent to one edge of the clearing. Although she had promised herself she would take no foolish risks, that this would only be a reconnaissance mission, Sara couldn't deny that a plan was beginning to form in her very weary, yet outraged, mind; a plan that was enticing for its simplicity.

Dawn would break soon. There was no time to waste.

"Hold on, Froggy," Sara whispered. "I'll help you. I *promise*."

12

KEEPING A WARY eye on the cracks and gaps in the Muckles' home in case anyone lit a lantern, indicating the inhabitants were stirring, Sara made her way to the base of the porch. Once she judged herself to be directly beneath the water barrel, she crouched in the oozing slime slowly dripping from the floor boards and unclasped the water-tight pouch from her belt. She dug through its scant contents, and her hand closed around the smooth surface of the jar of powdered cold-burrs. She allowed herself a small congratulatory smile at whatever premonition had prompted her to pack it before setting out on this journey.

In the dim light Sara looked at the jar of powder. Pale blue sparks glistened in its depths. Tipping and turning it, she estimated it was almost three-quarters full.

She tucked the jar into her jacket pocket. Placing one hand on the piling propping up that corner of the porch, she took an appraising look at the leaning length of soggy wood.

"Okay, Froggy," she breathed, "Wish me luck." With a small hop to give herself a boost, Sara climbed upward toward the leaky water barrel.

Wincing as her hands closed over splinters and scrabbling for a better purchase as the rubber soles of her tennis shoes slipped on the damp wood, Sara sent up a fervent prayer that no one would be awakened by her clumsy progress. Gripping the beam with forearms and thighs as tightly as she could, she managed to inch her way to the top. Breathing hard more from fear of being caught than from exertion, she leaned out, stretched up, and grabbed the edge of the porch floor with one hand. Slipping just a little, she transferred the other hand's grip to the floor board as well. After a moment's rest to gather her strength and to listen for any movement from within the Muckles' house, Sara pulled herself up until her hips cleared the level of the floor. With a soft thud that sounded like cannon fire to her anxious ears, she landed and dragged herself the rest of the way onto the porch. With the guilty speed of a trespasser, she crouched behind the protective cover of the water barrel. Her ears strained for any sound that would indicate she'd been found out, but all she heard was the sad, repetitive *thunk . . . thunk . . . thunk* of Froggy's confined misery.

A small corner of her mind, one she now thought of as "pre-swamp Sara," was crying out *What are you doing? Are you crazy? Are you totally nuts? Go back! Go back and wait for Granny to figure out what to do!* But as she peeked around the edge of the barrel, she saw something that made "post-swamp Sara" rage inside. Looking across the yard from her elevated vantage point, she made out three more makeshift pens like the one that enclosed poor Froggy.

Sara grew grim, and when the cautionary, pre-swamp voice whimpered again, her response was stern. "Oh, shut up. I'm not going back when I've come this far. What's the worst that could happen anyway?" *You could go missing like your Granddad Cal, that's what!* her pre-swamp self replied. *Think what that would do to Granny. Think of someone else for a change.* Sara leaned out a little further and watched Froggy rolling from side to side. From this height she could see the dark, velvety pools that she assumed were eyes. She marveled that a creature so featureless could convey such a look of pure tragedy. Breaking away from the sad sight, she gritted her teeth and sent pre-swamp Sara scuttling back to the far reaches of her mind where she belonged.

"I *am* thinking of someone else."

Using the barrel as partial shelter, she straightened enough to peer over the open top and into the murky darkness of the Muckles' home. The light was increasing as dawn approached, but she still couldn't discern more than vague shapes. There were lumpy piles of what looked like fabric scattered across the floor. She could see a metallic glint from what might be discarded, empty cans. A sudden scurrying widened her eyes and took her breath until she realized it was only a rat, probably investigating the cans for traces of food.

"Disgusting," she muttered and turned her attention back to the water barrel before her.

The floor on which Sara stood had suffered from the effects of the barrel's leakage. A soft, spongy rot threatened to dissolve the boards under her weight. Like a hiker negotiating a particularly tricky trail, inch by inch, she edged around to firmer footing. She was now in plain view of anyone passing through that level of the Muckles' home. With a nervous glance to assure herself there was still no sign of life other than that of the vermin variety, although she thought "vermin" an apt description of the human residents as well, she decided the risk of being seen was less than the certainty of it, if she crashed through the rotting floor.

Wincing at each faint, rusty squeak as she unscrewed the lid from the jar of cold-burr powder, Sara held it over the rim of the water barrel. Tipping it, her eyes widened with increasing anxiety as the cascade of sparkling blue she'd expected failed to materialize. Then she recalled that the jar was also sealed with paraffin. When she'd noticed the double seal back at Granny's cabin, she had applauded the added security as she stowed the jar in her pouch. Now, she frowned at the inconvenience of having to work the waxy plug out, wasting precious minutes during which she could be discovered. *Don't think about that,* she scolded herself, knowing nerves would only make her clumsy and slow, adding even more risk to her mission.

Narrowing her eyes, she tilted the jar toward the waking dawn and peered into it. There was a loop of cream-colored ribbon protruding above the wax disc sealing the mouth. Her damp fingers slid off the ribbon the first few times she tried to grip it. Biting her lip in frustration, she scrubbed her hand on her jeans, trying to achieve a drier touch. Grasping the fabric loop, she held the jar over the barrel of water and pulled as hard as she could.

The paraffin seal slid free with a gentle *pop*.

A hard, bony hand gripped Sara's shoulder with painful force.

The jar slipped from her fingers and sank to the bottom of the barrel, leaving a trail of glittering blue to dissipate in its wake.

"Well, well, well," a creaking voice snarled into her ear. "Malora! Malora, you lazy scum, wake up. We got ourself's a houseguest! Yes indeedy. Yes in*dee*dy."

Sara would have screamed, but terror closed her throat as effectively as the wax had stoppered the jar of cold-burr.

13

PANIC AND FEAR bouncing like marbles in her stomach, Sara looked up from the corner into which Saylish Muckle had thrown her. She rubbed her bruised shoulder. The grip from that horny, filthy hand had been surprisingly strong. She could feel the ache deep within the joint and tendons, but alarm and self-recrimination pushed the physical discomfort to the back of her thoughts. Saylish had tossed her like a rag doll and was now leering down at her, gloating over his captive as Malora hugged herself and pattered her dirty feet in a dance of gleeful anticipation.

"Well, well, well," Saylish crooned, leaning in close enough for Sara to smell fetid breath and to see the brown tobacco stain running from the corner of his mouth glisten with drool.

"What'cha doin' here, runt? Spyin' on us are ye?" Malora's incessant giggling ran beneath Saylish's tone of quiet violence.

"No!" Sara gasped, wondering if either had noticed her tampering with the water barrel.

She hadn't meant to pour the entire contents of the jar into it. She knew just from having brushed against the dried pods Granny had kept in her cupboard that cold-burrs were devastatingly effective. She had only hoped to add enough powder to their drinking water to make them sleepy. She had planned to watch, hidden at the swamp's edge, until they were groggy enough to be unaware of her presence. Then she would somehow rescue Froggy.

But Sara hadn't yet learned that wanting something with all your heart and soul didn't necessarily mean it would happen.

What was I thinking? I don't even know how much powder to use for that to happen. I should have waited for Granny. Now what'll they do to me? She could still hear the sad, methodical sound of Froggy rolling from side to side in the confinement of his pen. Regret welled up in Sara's chest, and she struggled to stifle the sob that rode it. *I'm sorry, Froggy. I meant to save you.*

Scowling, Malora stopped her little victory dance. With spider-like, crouching movements, she picked her way to the edge of the rotting porch and squinted into the swamp dawn. "Saylish! What if the old woman's here, too?"

"Naw, I don't think so. If'n she was here, she'd of made a ruckus by now with us takin' her little one. Abra-Lynn's too goody-goody to think of savin' herself." He licked his lips and tilted his head as he regarded Sara, who cowered as far away from him as she could.

"Now what'll we do with Abra-Lynn's little toad, Malora?"

"Take her out so far she'll never get back. Let the swamp have her, jes' like we done a-fore."

"Nope . . . uh-uh," Saylish drawled, clearly relishing the opportunity before him. "I mean *for fun.* Course we'll make sure she never sees her G-G-Gran again, but what we gonna do a-fore then? Hmmmm?"

He snapped his fingers and pulled an exaggerated face as though a brilliant idea had just that moment occurred to him. "I know. Let's make the little scum-toad help us grow our family first." Saylish's grin grew huge as he spit a brownish glob of thick liquid at Sara. It landed on the fingers of her hand that still rubbed her painful shoulder. She grimaced in revulsion, wiping the viscous substance on the grimy floor beside her as fast as she could. Saylish laughed and slapped his knees, smirking with self-congratulations.

"Don't ye think that'd be a grand thing, Malora, my love? To make the scum-toad help do what'll bring her Granny 'n' all her kind to her knees? Eh? Don't ye?"

Malora responded with additional gales of laughter. A tiny corner of Sara's mind that wasn't drowning in fear and remorse marveled at the amount of merriment that was part of the Muckles' twisted world. She'd never heard any two people laugh so much or so often. *They must be the life of the party when those bent on pushing the Source toward the bad side of the scales gets together*, she thought.

"Well! That's set then." Saylish grunted with satisfaction as he straightened up. Sara felt a little less crowded as he did; a respite that evaporated when he leaned around the corner of a doorway, reached for something, and stepped back into view grasping a solid-looking club.

"Here." He thrust the club toward Malora, who'd begun jigging about again, looking joyful as she savored the plans they'd made for Sara. "Take this and bop the toad good if'n she moves so much as a hair outta place."

Malora gripped the weapon in eager fingers, assuming a wide-legged stance right in front of Sara that made Sara take careful consideration of the logistics involved in keeping her hair absolutely still.

Saylish turned toward the water barrel, snapping his suspenders and rolling up his sleeves. "Big day ahead, Malora, my love. *Big* day. Best make ourselfs presentable-like."

Sara's thoughts erupted in turmoil above and beyond her own perilous situation. She wasn't sure if the amount of cold-burr powder she'd accidentally spilled into the water might kill Saylish if he drank it. Part of her jibbered with anger and fear that he deserved to die, given what he and Malora had probably already done to Granddad Cal and were planning to do to her. And diverting a soul or life essence or *whatever* Froggy was, from its rightful journey was a pretty terrible crime, too.

Let him drink the poisoned water.

But then the part of her that felt compassion for Froggy and was willing to risk everything to try and help took a firm stand. According to Granny, no one was sure *what* had happened to her grandfather. And so far she hadn't really been harmed. Maybe the Muckles were all talk. As for Froggy, Sara couldn't excuse them for the torment the poor creature was enduring at their hands, but she didn't know enough about this strange swamp world to make such a final judgment as to let someone drink what might possibly kill him; especially when *she* was the one responsible for rendering the water deadly in the first place.

When all was said and done, Sara realized the biggest crime that might come from all this could end up being committed by her hand. And how would something like that affect the rest of her life? Or Granny? Or even the Source, if she was connected to it already?

During the split second it took for this debate to rage through her, she saw Saylish step up to the water barrel and cup his hands together, ready to dip into the innocent-looking liquid.

In desperation, Sara bolted forward, disregarding Malora's screech of surprise as she made a clumsy swing with her club.

"Stop! Don't drink!" Sara shouted as she skittered under the moving club and slipped to one side, making frantic efforts to regain her footing on the slimy, plank flooring.

"Eh?" It was the only word Saylish managed before the club traversed a full half-circle, clipping the calf of his left leg. With a string of invectives, he fell to his knees. Malora lost her balance as well, landing beside him with a heavy thump, while the club completed its destructive arc, slamming into the soggy side of the water barrel.

Sara scrambled backward, looking cousin to a crab as she tried to make the most of this opportunity to escape. She hesitated for a brief moment as the barrel, side obliterated by the club's forceful impact, gushed its entire contents onto the Muckles, splashing across the length of the porch. It was amazing how much the leaky, old thing had held.

Sara pressed herself against the wall farthest from the side of the porch where the ruined barrel was still expelling bluish, glittering water. Although some dripped through the gapped and rotting floorboards, most of it pooled around Saylish and Malora.

"Ye stupid fool!" Saylish shouted, rubbing his injured calf. "I told ye to brain the toad if'n it moved . . . not me. Can't ye do anything right?"

"I tried! I didn' think she'd be dumb enough to do it! I . . ." Malora's whining trailed off. "Saylish! I can't feel my arms. My legs! They're goin' numb! *Saylish*!" Her voice took on a keening, terrified quality that raised the hair on Sara's neck.

"Wha' the . . . ? Somethin's in the water." Saylish rolled over, limp limbs flopping as his struggles sloshed more liquid onto himself and Malora.

Sara stared in horror before remembering her main objective was to escape and then try to help Froggy do the same. She flung herself toward the edge of the porch with its rotted railing. The drop was too far for a jump, but if she first lowered herself as much as she could by hanging onto the flooring, she should be able to avoid any serious consequences like broken bones or sprained ankles.

Casting a wary eye at the Muckles who were thrashing about in helpless anger, numb arms and legs flailing, Sara lowered herself down as far as her straightened arms allowed. As she dangled over the ground below, trying to work up the courage to let go, a few drops generated by the struggling, cursing couple landed on Sara's fingers. The decision to release her grip was no longer hers. A rushing, tingling sensation stole all feeling from her hands. With a startled grunt, she plummeted to the ground, landing with a thud, flat on her back.

14

IT TOOK SARA a moment to get her breath back and to realize that she hadn't suffered any serious injury from her fall. She looked at her hands in consternation, shaking them like limp gloves where they dangled from her wrists as she tried to coax feeling back into them. If the few stray drops that hit her had this immediate and powerful an effect, she couldn't imagine what Saylish and Malora were feeling . . . well, *not* feeling was perhaps more accurate.

She didn't know how long the numbness would last, so, scolding herself yet again for making plans without bothering to learn the crucial details that would spell the difference between success and failure, she lurched to her feet and looked around for Froggy.

The poor thing was still rolling from side to side, bumping up against the slats of the pen in which it was confined with a dull, hopeless sound, seemingly oblivious to the struggle that had taken place on the Muckles' porch. Sara approached with caution. Hands hanging at her sides, she knelt beside the soft, pinkish form.

Again, I don't know enough to be sure I'm doing the right thing.

But one thing of which she *was* certain was she couldn't abandon Froggy here. She chewed on her bottom lip, hoping some inspiration would strike, something that would tell her how to rescue a soul and where to take it if she did. She looked at the slats which formed Froggy's enclosure. They were tacked together with the same sloppiness that was the hallmark of the entire homestead. It was a testament to Froggy's helplessness that so little care had been put into making the pen sturdy. Peering a little closer, she could see markings scratched into the wood. They reminded her of the symbols on the clay discs that hung from Granny's porch rafters. She'd never bothered to ask about them, thinking they were just ornaments like wind chimes.

I should have asked about those things when I first came to visit instead of concentrating on being unpleasant company. Well, too late now.

With a disgusted sigh, Sara braced one forearm against the nearest board, hand dangling, and shoved. There was a screeching squeak of metal against wood, and the slat popped off. She gave it long, thoughtful regard. She stopped chewing her lip and a slow smile spread across her face.

Maybe there *was* a way to make everything work out for the best.

The second board was a bit more secure, but not by much. After a few pushes, it, too, tore loose. Sara was pleased that both pieces still had long, iron nails protruding from them where they'd been fastened to the posts forming the corners of the pen.

Froggy had stopped his disconsolate movements when Sara began dismantling the boards. She had the feeling that the creature was anticipating another jaunt with the Muckles; another journey of merciless prods and painful kicks. Her heart ached for the cruelty Froggy had endured.

"It's okay, Froggy," she crooned in what she hoped was a soothing manner, "I'm not like *them*. I'm trying to help you."

She cast a wary glance up at the Muckles. They were still flopping about, spewing angry, ineffectual curses. However, Sara noted that their speech had grown more slurred. She supposed their struggles had splashed some of the cold-burr water onto their lips. Despite whatever discomfort they might be experiencing, Sara was glad she couldn't really hear the invectives that she was sure were intended for her. She didn't know how long the effect of the numbing powder would last, but she knew it would be smart to hurry along as best she could.

She turned back to the boards from Froggy's pen and toed them about until they rested side by side with the long, rusty nails at each end pointing upward. She did a quick tour of the garbage and detritus strewn about the Muckles' yard. It didn't take her long to find what she wanted deep under the porch overhang. As luck would have it, it was on the far side from where the mishap with the water barrel had occurred, so there was no risk of doing any more damage to her hands, which had started stinging and tingling in ferocious waves of returning sensation.

I guess the feeling's coming back, she mused as she worked to free her find from under the porch. It was a dirty, frayed corner of fabric, but until she could excavate it from the debris surrounding it, she wouldn't know if it was truly suitable to the task she had in mind. Wrinkling her nose in distaste at the manner in which the Muckles chose to dispose of their garbage, she kicked as much of it off the fabric as she could. At last she exposed a sizeable piece of damp, muddy burlap.

Sara regarded her prize with a jaundiced eye. *Maybe Malora's saving this for a new dress*, she thought in a wry, uncharitable moment. It certainly did bear a resemblance to the filthy garment which draped Malora's bony frame. Sara clenched her jaw, trying to ignore the revulsion she felt at having to burrow about in the slimy mess under the Muckles' shack. She gripped the piece of cloth as tightly as she could between her wrists and yanked backward with all her strength. She managed to drag a few inches free before the wet burlap slipped from her grasp. Curling her lip at the streaks of muck her efforts had left on her skin and clothing, she backed out from under the porch.

This isn't working, she thought. *I need my hands or I'll be here forever. Think.* Frustration at her lack of manual dexterity and worry that the Muckles might find some way to recover before she did were uppermost in her mind, making calm reasoning and common sense very hard to access. The pouch she had tied to her belt when she'd set off on her own so many hours ago slapped against her thigh as she tried to work off some of her nervousness by pacing back and forth between the porch pilings. She came to a halt, eyes fastening on the lumpy pouch.

Wait! What if . . . ?

With speed born of urgency, Sara knelt and hooked her wrists about the pouch, bringing it around so it rested before her in her lap. When she had taken the jar of cold-burr powder from it, she hadn't fastened it closed. Sure enough, the pouch gaped open, it's only contents now were the crumpled, used foil in which she'd wrapped her food and the half-empty bottle of lemon-weed tea. She recalled yesterday when Granny had put her through her paces reciting the properties of lemon-weed and cold-burr. She had prompted Sara by asking her to consider the *opposite* of lemon-weed. Hardly daring to hope, Sara pushed at the pouch, trying to bring the bottle of tea into the open.

Could opposite mean antidote?

Sara fumbled at the stopper as the top of the bottle protruded upward from the pouch's mouth, making itself tantalizingly available, yet still a frustrating task for her mostly-numb fingers. She wasn't making any progress. Shaking her hair out of her eyes, she saw a rusty piece of scrap iron lying among the bits and pieces which littered the Muckles' yard. With a touch of regret for the faithful, old bottle, she lifted it, pouch and all, between her wrists and smashed it down on the hard edge of the iron. The force of the impact jarred her arms all the way up to her shoulders, but she grinned with satisfaction to hear the crunch of breaking glass and to see the flash of liquid pooling within the rubberized pouch.

It only took a moment for her to press the pouch flat against the ground, maneuvering the lemon-weed tea into a small puddle. Heart beating with frantic hope, Sara rested the fingers of one hand in the tea.

"Please work. Please," Sara begged.

At first she wasn't sure. It might have been wishful thinking. But, then, in a matter of minutes she *was* sure. Sensation was making a slow, painful return. Gritting her teeth against the pins-and-needles feeling, she allowed the fingers of both hands to rest in the lemon-weed infusion. It was a bit awkward since the pouch was still attached to her belt, but she managed. After several minutes which felt like hours as she listened to the sounds of the Muckles grunting and flopping about, Sara flexed her wrists and shook out her hands, pleased to feel the prickling lessen and normal sensation return.

She filed the experience away as a lesson concerning the power of cold-burr water. Then, she got busy.

She plunged back into the dark, dank recesses under the Muckles' porch. Swallowing her gag reflex and fumbling only a little, Sara grabbed the exposed piece of burlap and yanked at it until it came loose with a wet, tearing sound.

Grasping her hard-won, grimy treasure, she ran back to the boards from Froggy's pen. Stretching the burlap tight, she pushed the long, rusted nails through each corner of the fabric, creating a crude, cloth-covered frame that resembled a travois. Sara scrambled to the opposite, non-nail ends of the two boards and tucked an end under an arm apiece. Digging her heels into the muddy ground, she pulled the makeshift construction close to Froggy.

The poor creature remained very still as Sara dropped to her knees beside it. Worried, she crouched over the pinkish form. When it came down to it, she was reluctant to touch Froggy. Something felt so *wrong* about it.

Maybe once a soul is in this form, it isn't supposed to be touched by anyone . . . well, anyone not-dead. She shivered, and then gave herself a stern reminder that there was no time to waste. Even if Saylish and Malora remained incapacitated, Sara couldn't rid herself of the notion that Froggy's suffering would only be alleviated if he were allowed to continue his natural journey toward the Source. In addition, a corner of her mind was becoming more and more fretful about the worry her grandmother must be feeling. Full daylight poured into the clearing, so it was certain that Granny had discovered Sara's absence by now.

Taking a deep breath, Sara reached her arms around Froggy and tried to be gentle as she edged him closer to the rustic travois.

"It's okay, Froggy," she whispered. "I'm not going to hurt you. I'm here to help. I promise. I'll do my best. I promise, promise, promise . . ."

She kept up a constant stream of what she hoped were comforting words as she inched Froggy along. She was almost at a point where she could roll him onto the burlap when one of Froggy's eyes came into direct line with Sara's. Sara sucked in a sharp breath. She fell silent, soothing words forgotten.

Deep within the soft, velvety pool of the "eye" Sara thought she saw movement; fleeting images composed of iridescent grains which formed and reformed in faint, rainbow swirls. They appeared and disappeared in rapid succession, but Sara could have sworn she saw the semblance of a swamp-jenny or jack laughing and twirling in the deep darkness, then dissipating to form images of moss-hung branches, of the moon scudding among ragged clouds, of other places and things that could only be seen from deep within the bayou's heart.

Sara squeezed her eyes closed, trying not to become mesmerized by the flowing colors. She had no idea what, if any, meaning could be drawn from them. Was this the soul of a jenny or jack? Or were these things that had been witnessed by this particular soul at some point? The feeling of wrongness, of being privy to an aspect of existence meant to be kept separate from the solid world of the living shuddered through Sara's body. Steadying herself, she opened her eyes into Froggy's again and gave one last, firm tug that managed to roll the creature onto the travois.

When Froggy's eye broke contact, Sara cried out. Something had shot through her like the shock of an electrical surge. Thrown backward, she plopped onto the damp ground, catching her breath and blinking away the remnants of the images that had danced in the depths of Froggy's eyes. There was no time to ponder what it all could mean. Sara lurched to her feet, took a position between the bare boards that would serve as handles, lifted them up, and tucked them under her arms.

She pulled her burden with dogged determination over the rough ground to the edge of the clearing. A last look up to where the Muckles were still struggling brought a smile of grim satisfaction to her face.

All speech and cursing had ceased, but the sounds of Saylish and Malora rolling from side to side, thudding hollowly against the sodden porch railings was very like the sound Froggy had been making as he'd fetched up against the sides of his pen.

Poetic justice, thought Sara as she turned toward the swamp and began the long journey home . . . or wherever it would be appropriate to take a migrating soul.

"Okay, Froggy," she muttered. "Here we go. I'm not sure where, but here we go."

15

GRANNY WAS MAKING her way toward the patch of lemon-weed grass where she and Sara had encountered the Muckles. She tried to keep from imagining all the perils her granddaughter might meet, especially having set out at night, especially when it had been obvious that Sara's vision of the swamp night-glow had been diminishing. Yet, even when Granny could keep her fretful imagination under control, she couldn't stop replaying her memories.

Granny recalled a similar flight so many years ago. She had set off in the same direction she now traveled, but then she had been spurred on by the disappearance of her husband, Cal. She had been sure the Muckles had something to do with Cal's fate. She still didn't know precisely what that was, but she'd learned to trust her instincts when it came to matters concerning those closest to her heart.

She still felt fatigued, which told her the Source remained unbalanced. Thinking of Cal added a deep ache. Thinking that she might lose Sara as well was unbearable. Unnoticed, a slow tear inched down her weathered cheek.

They took my Cal. I'm sure of it. I can't let them take my Sara-Jean. She pushed on through the marshy terrain.

Hours later, she reached the lemon-weed patch. The sun had warmed the grasses enough to release their bright, citrus fragrance. Granny took a seat by the same gnarled, old oak that had sheltered them yesterday. She plucked a stem of the bright yellow grass and chewed it absently, begrudging herself even this short rest.

The juices of the lemon-weed were therapeutic. She felt a little better, a trifle less dejected. But as she rose to continue her journey, she stopped short. Holding very still, she closed her eyes to shut out any visual distraction, wondering if what she was feeling was real or just the effect of lemon-weed and wishful, hopeful thinking.

No. It's definite. I know this too well to be fooled at my age.

A slow smile crept over her face as she opened her eyes. No doubt about it. There was a change in how she felt; a soul-deep shifting that she had known many times before when her attempts to re-balance the Source had been successful. Whatever had happened, something was working toward restoring the *status quo*.

The girl could still be in danger, but she must've done somethin' right, Granny decided. She shook her head and marveled at the impulse she suddenly felt to send a loud, joyful cheer echoing through the swamp. Sara had surpassed her hopes and expectations already. If she had managed to correct an imbalance, particularly one as grievous as the Muckles had imposed, there was no telling what powers the girl might achieve in time.

Land sakes. This here's no time for lolly-gaggin', Granny scolded herself. *Only an old fool would take it for granted that things couldn't swing back to wickeder than worse. Get movin', old woman.*

With a lighter heart and a sprier step, Granny clambered across the old oak's roots and continued on toward Saylish and Malora's home.

With a hurried plea to Granddad Cal's spirit to watch over the granddaughter he'd never met, Granny plunged on through the wilderness of twisting vines and dripping mosses.

16

AFTER A WEARY hour of dragging her homemade travois through the swamp, Sara was ready to admit that she'd been all wrong. She had thought that springing Froggy from the clutches of the Muckles would be the most demanding, most difficult part of this whole endeavor. Now she realized that she hadn't reckoned on her own physical state of sleepless, famished exhaustion once the main task had been achieved.

Maybe because I've never been allowed to stay up all night or skip meals or hike for miles on my own, let alone do all three at once, she thought as she paused to shake lank, sweaty hair out of her eyes. She surveyed the terrain before her with a sinking feeling that had only a little to do with the fact that the added weight of transporting Froggy made her feet, well . . . *sink* into soggy ground that would have let her stay high and dry, if she'd been unhindered. She'd never noticed before how lumpy and uneven the land really was. Walking over it with nothing to carry other than a pouch containing her lunch, a jar of cold-burr powder, and a bottle of lemon-weed tea had allowed her to be blissfully unaware of its irregularities.

She glanced back at Froggy who had been curiously still since she'd hefted him onto the burlap stretched between the boards. She couldn't decide if it was the lightening day or a consequence of being freed by a friendly force, but Froggy seemed to be rosier and more glowing than when he . . . she? . . . it? . . . had been a captive.

I wonder if he knows he's been rescued, Sara mused. Whatever the reason, she decided it was a good sign and took it as encouragement that she was doing the right thing for Froggy's welfare.

She hitched the boards more securely against her ribs, gave a weary sigh, and scanned the path ahead. She'd never been so tired and hungry, yet at the same time, she'd never felt a greater sense of pride and accomplishment. She wondered if Granny felt the same rewarding glow whenever she worked to protect the Source's balance. In a way, she could understand a little better now how her grandmother managed to enjoy such a solitary, almost primitive life. That reminded her that the time when she would have to choose where her own path would lead was fast approaching. Would she choose the same life? And thinking of paths in general reminded her that standing here panting and sweating wouldn't help either Froggy or herself, or make that inevitable time of decision any easier.

Sara lowered her head and, straining forward, struggled toward what she judged to be the least difficult path, even though it harbored a discouraging number of tussocks and boggy spots.

17

SARA HAD NO idea how much time had passed when noises penetrated the fog of exhaustion surrounding her. She wasn't sure how long the sounds had been approaching while she toiled on, unaware of anything other than placing one foot in front of the other, but this was not the background noise of moisture and furtive life that was so natural it could be ignored.

She stopped in her tracks. It sounded like the progress of a large creature. And it was getting uncomfortably close. Could Saylish and Malora have recovered from the cold-burr's numbing power and be pursuing her? Could they travel quickly enough to overtake her? Sara had to admit that the burden of Froggy had slowed her considerably. She also had to acknowledge that the Muckles were long-time residents of the swamp and likely had antidotes for cold-burr at their disposal, too. Swamp-craft was where she herself was sorely lacking. It could be that the Muckles had all manner of ways and means of which Sara was woefully ignorant.

Once again she kicked herself for her arrogance in assuming she could wander off half-cocked and set everything right on her own.

No time for regrets now. If I ever get through this and see Granny again, I swear I'll listen more and think more and dive in head first a lot *less.*

Exhaustion and the strange acoustics of the swamp rendered Sara's hearing directionless. She couldn't tell from where the sounds were coming. She looked around for someplace to hide, but there was no way she could conceal both herself and Froggy before whomever or whatever it was would be upon them.

Moving as quickly as her tired limbs and tired mind could manage, she released her grip on the travois boards and grabbed the rubberized pouch still hanging in a limp lump from her belt. She widened its opening, tilting the dark interior toward the sunlight. Deep inside, bright reflections winked as the sun's rays glanced off the remnants of the shattered bottle that had contained lemon-weed tea.

With ginger care, Sara reached into it and extracted a particularly long, jagged shard of glass. A bit of silver filigree that had ornamented the bottle was still fastened to one end. She gripped it like the hilt of a dagger. Straddling the inert form of Froggy, feeling grim and protective, she brandished her weapon before her. Unsure of where her opponent might materialize, she scanned in all directions. Impromptu dagger held high, Sara bared her teeth, trying to look fierce and formidable. She tried to ignore that she was bedraggled, begrimed, and just plain scared.

18

HUMMING A LITTLE walking song to herself, Granny pushed her way through an unusually tall stand of rushes. The dried stalks rattled and clattered against one another. She'd been watching the ground in an effort to avoid stepping into one of the marshy depressions that seemed to pepper this stretch of land more so than most. She emerged from behind the rushes. Once sure of her footing, she looked up.

And stopped short.

There was Sara, looking like some kind of ancient swamp-spirit, face and hair streaked with mud, a ferocious grimace transforming her normally gentle features, and waving what looked like a splinter of glass.

After a moment of shock, chased by surprise and relief, Granny burst into laughter.

"Land sakes, child. I've been worried sick and here you are lookin' fit to scare the daylights out of anyone with sense enough to see. Land sakes." She continued to laugh in what Sara and her bruised dignity now considered an unwarranted amount of merriment.

Adrenaline ebbing, Sara abandoned her battle stance.

"Gran! You scared the *life* out of me. I thought Saylish and Malora were hunting me down, and I'd never see you again. Stop laughing."

"Girl, you should be glad I'm a-laughin' instead of tearin' you limb from limb for doin' such a darn fool thing as settin' out on your own." Granny wiped tears from her eyes and came closer, wanting to be certain her potential apprentice, and a little girl she loved very much, was undamaged. With gentle care, she relieved Sara of the glass shard and grasped both of her hands in a tight hold. "Sara-Jean, child, are you alright?"

For a moment Sara could only gaze at her grandmother's face. That weathered, lovely, *loveable* face. Bruises, bumps, and fatigue aside, Sara realized that the thing that had worried her most through her hours of struggle and fear hadn't really been the rescue of Froggy or the importance of restoring balance to the Source. What had sat in a dark corner of her mind all along was the fear that she would never see her Granny again, or sit on the porch steps, listening to stories and swamp-lore the like of which would never be voiced under the harsh glare of electric light in the pristine, modern kitchen of her parents' home.

I wonder when I stopped resenting her and began to love her, Sara mused.

When she recalled her original reluctance to even *meet* her mother's mother, she felt a twinge of shame. How brave Granny was for setting aside material comforts and the solace of her own family's daily presence in order to devote herself to a higher cause. And such a strange cause. Caretaking the Source wasn't something Granny could explain to just anyone, Sara realized. If she tried, she would no doubt be labeled eccentric at best, crazy at worst.

Sara thought of the people she sometimes saw wandering about with aimless, blank eyes on the streets of Baton Rouge, mumbling to themselves, avoided by passersby because they were odd and made others feel uncomfortable. Suddenly she had a vision of Granny roaming the hard pavement of civilization, ignored and spurned as she muttered stories about this peculiar, this *beautiful* swamp world. And then, as Sara watched the vision playing out before her mind's eye, Granny's face became her own.

If I choose my home, my family, my friends, I'll have to abandon all the wonders I've seen here. I won't even be able to talk about this or everyone will think I'm nuts.

A kind of quiet horror washed over Sara as she finally understood the absolute finality of whichever path she chose. There would be no traveling back and forth. There would be no pleasant, easy blending of the outside world and the secrets of the bayou. *So that's why Mama never comes back here to where she grew up. That's why Granny never comes to visit.*

In the end you can't belong to both places.

19

"CHILD?" GRANNY WAS peering at Sara, concern etched in the lines that creased her brow and radiated from her eyes.

The sudden sympathy for her grandmother's life, her mother's own choice, and the gravity of her own looming decision, lumped on top of being just plain worn out with the night's adventures was finally too much. Sara burst into tears.

"Sara-Jean, what's wrong? Are you hurt?" Granny released Sara's hands and did a quick scan of her for any obvious wounds or injuries. There didn't seem to be anything seriously wrong, so Granny pushed the lank, muddy hair away from Sara's eyes and took hold of her chin, tilting her face up to her own.

"Child, I'm not happy with how you ran off on your own, but listen to me now." Something in Granny's tone made Sara gulp down her tears, take a deep, shuddering breath, and try to look past her whirling thoughts.

"Like I said, Sara-Jean, I'm not happy about the *how* of what you've done, but I'm right proud of the *what*. Fact is, I don't know what you've been through, but I do know when the Source tells me things have been set right. I know you're probably feelin' poorly, but we got some distance to cover yet. Now, let's head for home and you can tell me what you've been up to out here all on your own." Granny dusted her hands off in a no-nonsense manner and turned back toward the way she'd come.

Sara blinked in confusion. "But Granny! What about Froggy? We can't just leave him here."

Granny looked back over her shoulder at the softly glowing mass ensconced on Sara's travois.

"Land sakes, child. What do you think happens when something passes on a-way out here? You think there's some kinda taxi cab service comes and collects its soul?" Granny chuckled, which took any sting out of the admonishment.

Sara took a few steps closer to the burlap travois and bent over Froggy. Even through her weariness, she felt an air of quiet serenity emanating from the creature. She avoided looking into its "eyes." She had no desire to be bewitched yet again by the flowing images she'd seen last time.

"Sara-Jean, come away from there." There was a note of urgency in Granny's command, but Sara just couldn't turn her back after all she'd been through on the poor soul's behalf.

"Froggy, will you be okay?" she asked; the words as soft as the morning breeze.

The rose-pink form seemed to pulse. Sara wondered if that was its way of answering her.

"Child! I said to come here." Anger and alarm warred in Granny's voice.

"Froggy, I have to leave now," Sara whispered. "I'm sorry for everything you've been through, but I did my best to make it right."

More pulsations chased across the soul's fuzzy surface. Sara could almost, almost discern other colors besides the dominant pink tone.

"Sara-Jean!" There was no mistaking Granny's displeasure with her lingering farewell now.

Sara decided she'd better heed her grandmother's call. But it was so hard to turn away. The feeling of near revulsion she'd first experienced when she had to move Froggy onto the burlap travois back at the Muckles' seemed an insubstantial memory now. She reached one hand toward the rosy mass, wanting to let it know with a touch that she regretted Saylish and Malora's cruelty, that she wished it well and hoped it now had a safe journey to the Source, if that's where it was truly headed.

Granny's strong, work-hardened hand closed around Sara's wrist in an iron grip.

"Stop it, girl." Granny yanked her away, pulling her from Froggy's side and herding her none too gently toward the path home. At the last moment, Granny turned back, brow furrowed as she scanned the boards lying on each side of Froggy. With speed born of urgency, she flipped them over so the symbols carved into them lay against the ground; no longer visible.

"Child, when I tell you to do something, you *do* it, hear?" She resumed hurrying Sara along. "You may have learned a lot, young lady, but there's a whole passel more you don't know. So when someone like me, who's been around a sight longer than you have, tells you to do somethin', you'd best pay attention."

"I was only saying 'goodbye,'" Sara protested. She stumbled as Granny pushed her forward, still craning over her shoulder, trying to catch a last glimpse of Froggy.

"Land sakes. I never heard such swamp-ooze," Granny exclaimed. "I'll admit you're seein' and doin' some things I never did at your age, girl, but you *mind* what you're told and do *what* you're told *when* you're told or it might not matter if you choose to be a swamp-witch or city-bred 'cause you'll be *dead*! Understand?"

Sara looked properly sheepish despite still harboring the private opinion that she hadn't been in any danger or doing any harm by lingering beside Froggy. Granny seemed to be aware of her rebellious thoughts. Taking Sara's upper arm, she hustled her over to the tall stand of rushes from which she'd made her entrance. Granny crouched behind the stalks, pulling Sara down beside her.

"Now keep still and watch, girl. Maybe you'll be reminded to keep an open mind and open eyes, like I been tellin' you for nigh on five years now." Grumbling to herself, Granny fidgeted about, settling into a more comfortable position. Chastened, Sara held her tongue and strained to see over a rather large tussock to where Froggy's glow seemed to be brightening.

Minutes dragged by, and Sara shifted position, giving subtle vent to her impatience. Taking a sidelong look at Granny, she decided to risk prodding her with a question. "Gran?"

"Hush up, girl," Granny said in a terse voice. "You want to know why I wouldn't let you settle down and have a good, long chin-wag with that soul, then hush up and keep your eyes open."

Resigned, Sara let her mind wander back over the previous night's deeds. She wondered if Saylish and Malora were still paralyzed by the cold-burr powder, or if they'd managed to escape the situation and were even now trailing after her in the hope of recapturing their "son," Froggy. She heard a sudden commotion of snapping twigs and what sounded like several heavy weights being dragged through the dried grasses and pursuit sprang to mind.

"Gran!" Sara's hiss was sharp, frantic, as she looked from side to side, trying to pinpoint the direction from which she was sure the Muckles would make an appearance.

"Hush," Granny said. Her voice was softer. There was no fear or alarm underlying her instructions this time. Having already been scolded for not doing as she was told, Sara held very still and waited, keeping Froggy in view as best she could.

Some*thing* emerged, forcing its way through the bracken and undergrowth. Or rather, five some*things* emerged. Sara squeezed her eyes shut for a moment, wondering if fatigue and hunger were affecting her vision. She looked again. The creatures were still converging on Froggy and hadn't changed their appearance in the least.

Sara decided the best way to describe them was a cross between a large snake like the pictures she'd seen of pythons or anacondas, and the limb of a tree. Each of the five seemed to have a blunt, club-shaped head which tapered back for at least fifteen feet until it ended in a rounded point. Their skins looked rough and mottled brown, resembling bark more than anything else. From their heads to just past their mid-sections, their backs and sides were covered with small, twig-like projections, most of which jutted out at forty-five degree angles. Sara couldn't see any indication of eyes, ears, or mouths. The things looked like sinuous, moving branches.

"Granny, what are they?" Sara whispered, keeping her eyes fixed on the creatures' progress.

"Serpentrees," her grandmother replied, giving the first letter of the word a rattling, sibilant sound. "Just watch, girl."

The five creatures moved in, converging on Froggy's glowing form, their blunt heads inches from him. After a moment of being silent and still, they gathered into a small circle alongside the travois, tail sections pointed outward. Sara saw them lift their heads and most of their bodies skyward. In curving, bobbing movements more graceful than she would have expected from what resembled animated logs, the five wove their bodies together, braiding themselves into an upward-reaching column. The maneuver was accomplished in a matter of seconds, the twiggy lengths making cracking noises as they slapped against each other.

Fascinated, Sara realized that she might have passed these creatures a number of times during her summer visits to the swamp without recognizing them. In the end, what loomed before her looked like a tree with a twisted trunk the crown of which branched out into five thick limbs. The twiggy projections and bark-like skin would never have given the creatures' true nature away to a casual observer. The final touch to the serpentrees' disguise was given by their tapered tails. Stretching out from the braided "trunk," they looked exactly like the roots of so many other trees one found in the swamp; partially above ground with tips that dipped beneath the surface. Sara shuddered as she wondered if she'd ever used the tail of a serpentree as a convenient seat during her wanderings, or leaned her back against a twiggy trunk that wasn't *really* rooted in the soil.

Sara's fascination with the serpentrees broke when she noticed a change in Froggy. The soul's glowing pink color flared, coruscating tones of red washing over its surface. The color peaked into painful brightness, but then seemed to ebb and soften again. Trails of rosy luminescence seeped across the ground from Froggy to the tail-tips of the serpentrees. Several minutes later, pinkish waves shuddered upward along the woody lengths. As the colors faded, each twig-like protrusion burst forth with what Sara thought resembled small blossoms with softly glowing, pink petals.

"Ohhhh," Sara breathed as she watched the transformation. "Oh, Gran, they're *beautiful.*"

Before she felt she'd had time to fully appreciate them, the serpentrees lifted their heads upward and unbraided themselves in a graceful, waving dance, becoming five distinct creatures again. Twigs still bearing their pale, pink burdens, the five writhed across the ground in close formation. As they disappeared into the undergrowth with loud rustling and dragging sounds, Sara looked back at her travois.

No sign of Froggy remained.

The crunching, grinding noise of the serpentrees' departure grew fainter and fainter.

When only the normal sounds of the swamp fell on their ears in gentle cadence, Granny rose from their vantage point behind the rushes. Dusting herself off, she peered up at what was visible of the sky and sighed.

"Come on, girl. Day's a-wastin'. Let's head home."

20

WEARY, SARA WAS content to trail along in Granny's wake. At first they hiked in silence, both too preoccupied with the strange absorption of a life force that they had just witnessed to give much thought to conversation.

Granny's musings bounced between several different levels as she trudged ahead, keeping an eye on Sara to be sure she didn't lag too far behind. Along with mundane concerns like getting home, making Sara dinner, and then hustling her into bed, Granny was touching on some more serious subjects. She was curious to know the details of Sara's adventures for a number of reasons. Chief among those were ascertaining just how quickly the Muckles could be counted on to seek revenge. It was possible that they would simply lick their wounds and savor their indignation without taking any further action. It was also possible that they would escalate their capture of souls in a flurry of angry vengeance, even if they didn't aim their malice directly at Granny or Sara.

She also wanted specifics about everything Sara had done, because the girl was still too inexperienced to know the consequences of all her actions.

Look how she wanted to linger by that Froggy without knowin' about serpentrees. And I'm bettin' she had no compr'hension that those runes scratched on the boards where what kept the serpentrees away long as they was visible. And she prob'ly doesn't know they're part of a language of power and keep my little home safe from all kinds of perilous things long as I keep them etched on my charms and amulets; keep 'em fresh and swingin' over the porch. And look how she wanted to touch a soul essence without knowin' what it could do to a body. Land sakes . . .

On top of everything else, Granny was all too aware that Sara's visit would end the day after tomorrow.

The girl knows enough to make a choice, but I sure couldn't say what it'll be with all the goin's-on we've had this time 'round.

They reached the lemon-weed patch that Granny estimated as a rough half-way mark between Saylish and Malora's ruined shack and her own homely cabin.

"Let's rest here, child," she said when Sara caught up to her. "Set a spell and get a second wind."

They made themselves comfortable among the familiar, old oak's roots. Granny smiled when she saw Sara take a very close look at the roots and the ancient trunk towering above them.

"Don't worry, girl. Serpentrees ain't *that* big. Leastways, not any I've ever seen."

When they were seated, Granny reached out and plucked several stems of the yellow reeds surrounding them. She handed a couple to Sara, leaned back with a thoughtful expression, and chewed on the succulent roots. Sara followed her example, expelling a sigh of relief at how much better she felt thanks to the virtues of this unassuming little weed.

After a few minutes, Granny broached one of the worries on her mind.

"So, Sara-Jean, you 'bout ready to fill me in on what you been up to?"

Sara blew another gusty sigh and recounted the tale of Froggy's rescue, beginning with an apology for sneaking out in the middle of the night, ending with her determination to protect the lost soul with her impromptu glass dagger, and her relief when Granny had emerged from the bracken instead of Saylish and Malora.

Granny nodded, but said nothing. After a short time, they continued on their homeward trek. Reinvigorated somewhat, Sara managed to keep pace with her grandmother and continued fleshing out the details of her rescue mission. When she recalled the mesmerizing images she'd seen in Froggy's eye and the odd jolt she'd felt when moving him onto the travois, Granny interrupted and made her go over it again.

"And mind you be givin' me as accurate and detailed a tellin' as still lives in your mind, child. No matter if tiredness be cloudin' your mem'ry."

"Why's it so important?" Sara sounded querulous after wracking her mind for anything she might have left out the first two times she repeated this particular part of her adventure. Her patience was wearing thin as her hunger and weariness increased.

"Don't rightly know that it *is* important, girl." Granny cast a sympathetic look at Sara who stumbled over a protruding cypress root.

"C'mon, Gran. Spill it." Sara couldn't restrain a cavernous yawn despite her curiosity.

"Well, there's not much to spill. To tell you the truth, the closest I've ever been to a soul on its travels was today when I stood a few feet off from that Froggy of yours. Never looked one in the eye. Never touched one." Granny chose her next words with care. "But I have heard some tales and rumors over the years."

"What?" Vague alarm crept into Sara's voice. "What kind of tales and rumors?"

"Now, now," Granny said in a soothing tone. "Nothin' for certain or sure. Just tales about folk bein', well, *changed* by such-like . . . by touchin' a soul."

Sara stopped in her tracks and fixed her grandmother with a horrified stare. "Gran! What's *that* supposed to mean? Am

I going to turn all pink and fuzzy like Froggy? Am I going to sprout wings or warts or . . . *what?*"

Despite Sara's urgency, Granny couldn't help but chuckle, a sound which took the edge off of Sara's concern. "Nothin' like that, girl. Nothin' so *visible. If* the tales are true, and mind you, I'm not sayin' they *are,* then communin' that closely with a travelin' soul might leave its mark on you by way of givin' you a special talent. A gift you might say. Could be somethin' totally new, could be increasin' somethin' you already have. Might be nothin' at all." Her tone lowered. "Might be somethin' you don't want."

"Ohhh great," Sara groaned. "I'm tired, Granny. These last few days have been really cool, you know? But I could use some down time right about now." She sighed and resumed following in Granny's wake through the darkening swamp. "So now what do I do?"

"Nothin'. No point in worryin' about what might never be, girl."

They walked on for a time.

"But, Sara-Jean, there is somethin' more you *should* know." Granny's tone told Sara that this might be important.

This might be yet another bit of information that should be added to a store of knowledge that was already growing too quickly. Sara felt as though her brain was about to burst with the changes and unexpected events of the last few days.

"Tell me, Gran."

"The gifts you already have are enormous, child. More than anyone could have guessed. Whether or not touchin' Froggy gave you more doesn't really matter right now. When you go back to your home, back to school and all, you won't fit in quite the way you used to. The only place you'll fit in and still use all those talents will be here. If you choose to follow your mama's way, you'll have to forget about all this. You'll have to ignore those gifts. You'll have to *un*learn what you've picked up visitin' me."

Granny fell silent, hoping she had made the consequences of Sara's decision clear without unduly affecting it. Privately, she hoped it would make her granddaughter find the swamp-ways just that much more enticing.

21

BY THE TIME they reached the weathered, old cabin the sun had set.

Despite her depleted physical condition, Sara smiled. The night-glow was back; every feature, every detail etched in lovely, opalescent, green fire. If anything, it was brighter than Sara had seen it before. She watched her grandmother leading the way and acknowledged that there was still energy and vitality in her movements after her long day's search for Sara.

The Source must be back on track, she thought. *And maybe it's even tilted a little bit more toward our side than before.*

She remembered Granny telling her that leaning to either side too much wasn't the best position for the Source, but she couldn't help a certain smug contentment. *It feels like we won.*

They clambered up the worn, porch steps and divested themselves of mud-encrusted outerwear, which, in Sara's case was most of her clothing.

"Get washed-up, child," Granny instructed. "I'll rustle up somethin' to eat and then it's bed for us both."

Sara dragged the deep, tin bathtub out to the porch where a huge water barrel stood. She was glad to note that Granny's container was in much better condition than the soggy, shabby version that the Muckles had possessed. In fact, after trespassing on Saylish and Malora's property, she was rather proud of how her grandmother maintained her house and land. *Rustic*, Sara decided. *But not decrepit. Worn, but not filthy.*

Too tired to bother with heating the water, she ladled the tub half full and gratefully slid into the tepid liquid. Just as she realized that she'd forgotten to bring some of Granny's homemade soap with her, a smooth, square chunk of it was lobbed from inside the cabin, splashing into her bathwater.

"Thanks, Gran!" Sara called, losing no time in working up a fragrant lather. In past years she hadn't bothered to ask her grandmother about the art of making soap. Now she was surprised to find herself wondering just exactly how the grainy substance scented with flowers and herbs was produced.

I guess my mind is a little more open than when I first came here, she admitted. *Actually, there's a lot I wish I'd asked about before. I've wasted so much time.*

Feeling a little mournful at her newfound perspective and feeling a lot hungry, Sara wrapped herself up in the threadbare, floor length robe Granny let her use whenever she came to stay. She emptied the bathwater over the edge of the back porch and noticed, for the first time, a rope that was tied to the rail and disappeared into the water, anchored by something heavy enough to resist being moved by currents.

I must really be out of it, she yawned. *I don't even feel like asking what that is.*

She ambled indoors and saw Granny had managed to assemble sandwiches which were toasting on a rack over the fire. The savory aroma told her they likely contained salted meat and a sharp cheese. In addition, a pot of hearty bean soup was simmering.

"Sit down, girl," Granny commanded.

Sara was only too glad to comply. She sighed with satisfaction as a sandwich with warm, crusty bread, oozing melted cheese and the sweet juices of a thick slice of ham was placed before her. A large cup of rich, steaming soup followed. Granny slid into her chair opposite Sara's and echoed her sigh.

For a good half hour the two ate at a steady pace, replenishing depleted reserves. When the edge of hunger had been blunted, Granny wrapped her hands around her still-warm cup of soup and regarded Sara with grave concern. Sara continued to work at demolishing her dinner.

"Sara-Jean, I expect we'll both sleep late, but tomorrow we'll have to make good use of what time is left. Since you have a real important decision to make, I'll let you say how you'd like to spend your last hours here."

Sara detected a sorrowful undertone to Granny's pronouncement. She was so tired that she'd managed to push the dreaded time of choosing off to the side of her thoughts. But Granny had dragged it back to the forefront, and there was no avoiding its inevitability now.

"I'll just tell you one thing, child," Granny continued. "I won't be sayin' any more on the subject. The way it works from here on is that you'll have to make up your mind on your own without anyone tryin' to make you say 'yea' or 'nay.' I'll answer any more of those nonstop questions you seem so full of, but I can't help you choose your path."

Sara gulped down the mouthful of bread she'd been chewing. "But you want me to choose *you*, don't you, Granny?"

"Doesn't matter what I want, girl. This is *your* life we're talkin' about." With that, Granny began to clear the dishes away. "Time for bed now."

Sara turned a blank, unfocused gaze on the surface of the wood plank table, considering the consequences of her options. All she knew was that she was too tired to analyze; too overwhelmed to follow any line of reasoning to a satisfactory conclusion. She rose in automatic obedience, shambled to her bed, and slipped under the thin, coarsely woven blanket. She listened to Granny make her own nighttime preparations and heard the rustling noises the mossy stuffing made as she, too, lay down on her pallet across the room.

"Go to sleep, child." Granny's soft command drifted to Sara, barely louder than the gentle, rhythmic noises of water lapping at the pilings of the back porch.

The last thing Sara remembered before a deep, dreamless slumber pulled her into its depths was the sudden sharp realization that she hadn't done anything during her rescue mission to discover how the Muckles had managed to hijack poor, luckless Froggy from traveling to the Source.

Nor had anything been done to prevent them from doing so again.

22

SARA WOKE AND the first thing she did was groan. Every bump and bruise, every scratch and scrape assured her that she hadn't dreamt her adventure, nor any of the physical insults that had accompanied it. As she took inventory of each part of her body that ached, stung, or throbbed, she regretted not having taken the time to heat her bathwater the night before.

Grimacing, she propped herself up on her elbows and scanned the cabin for Granny. Although she wasn't present, Sara could hear a combination of splashing and slapping sounds coming from the front yard. The sight and aroma of freshly baked muffins piled high on a plate on the kitchen counter next to a rectangular lump draped in cheesecloth was tempting enough to make her force her body to a sitting position. Taking a deep breath in anticipation of the protest her muscles would register, she swung her legs around and placed both feet on the floor, ready to take a solid stance.

Good grief, even the soles of my feet hurt. She winced and decided making her way into the kitchen area might be all she was capable of accomplishing for the day. By the time she dragged on some clean jeans and a t-shirt, her body wasn't complaining quite so much. Encouraged, she did a few experimental stretches and had to admit that her initial thought about staying in bed was open for debate.

With still-ginger movements, Sara made her way to the kitchen counter. She discovered the length of cheesecloth covered a large, golden slab of butter. She lost no time applying some of the creamy spread to a muffin and taking it out to the front porch where the watery slapping sounds continued.

Halfway across the yard Granny was vigorously rubbing the clothing Sara had muddied on her trek against an old-fashioned washing board. As with the production of soap, Sara realized she'd never paid much attention during her two-week visits to most of the mundane tasks that were part and parcel of daily, uneventful, bayou life. She felt a little guilty, watching her grandmother cleaning up after her. Somehow, at home with her parents, it didn't bother her at all when Mama did her laundry.

Maybe it's because this looks like so much work, she thought. *At home it's just a matter of dumping stuff into a machine and pushing a button. I wonder if I could get used to living without all those things that make chores so much easier.*

"Good morning, Gran!" she called as she crossed the porch to the top of the steps, muffin in hand. "Can I help?"

"No, thank-ye kindly, girl," Granny replied, glancing up from her bent position over the soapy water. "You just have your breakfast and consider what you want to know or do on your last day. I'm almost done here anyway."

She gave the socks she was scrubbing one last dip in the water before wringing them out. With a brisk movement she shook them and strode to one side of the yard where a length of rope was stretched taut between the limbs of one of the odd, black, holly trees that stood over the house like sentinels. With a practiced snap, she flipped the socks over the rope and left them to dry in the sun. Judging by the number of items draped over the rustic laundry line, Sara realized Granny must have been up and about for quite some time already. Enough time to clean two weeks' worth of clothing for both herself and Sara, and to bake muffins for breakfast.

Sara did as Granny instructed and turned her attention to the still-warm, corn muffin, colored even a brighter yellow from having absorbed the large pat of butter Sara had slathered onto it. She bit through the crunchy top and was surprised to find the slight heat of jalapeno peppers had been mixed into the batter. She closed her eyes and chewed, reflecting that the pleasant burn woke her up more thoroughly than a sip of Granny's bitter bark tea or a dip in the chilly water from the rain barrel before sunshine had had a chance to warm it.

As she ate, Sara watched Granny empty the used water from the washtub, wipe off the washboard, and prop both at an angle against the bottom of the steps where the sun would dry them. She noted her grandmother wasn't particularly talkative this morning, nor was she making much eye contact with Sara.

She's letting me make up my own mind, just as she said she would. The thought of her impending decision, this life-altering choice looming over her, stole the savor from her breakfast and reduced what she'd already eaten to a heavy lump of anxiety in her stomach. Sara regarded the remnants of her muffin with a distinct lack of enthusiasm. She set the uneaten portion atop the porch railing and brushed her hands across her denim-clad knees to rid them of any buttery, clinging crumbs.

"Gran?"

"Yes, child?" Granny gave the drying laundry one last appraising look before turning to face her granddaughter.

"Why do I have to choose now? Why can't I just keep on coming out to see you in the summer? Maybe stay longer than two weeks?" Sara tried to pitch her voice in a persuasive, reasonable tone that she hoped would sway Granny into allowing her to postpone the inevitable decision.

"Well, girl, it's like this." Granny took a seat on the steps beside Sara, lowering herself to the worn boards with a sigh. "Once you've seen the laputa birds, the swamp starts to mark you. Now, most people see the laputas a coupla' times and have to choose at that point. You've already seen and done a *lot* more than that." She took a moment to gaze out at the warm, peaceful bayou stretching beyond her front yard.

"Seein' things like you have, openin' your eyes and your mind, isn't somethin' you can leave behind when you go back city-way. I'm already worried 'bout you fittin' in and bein' normal if you choose to stay back there."

Sara gave Granny a sidelong, skeptical look.

Her grandmother took a deep breath and leaned forward, resting her elbows on her knees. "Child, do you know what the best musicians and the best dancers and the best at speakin' lots of diff'rent languages and the best at, oh, I don't know . . . *lots* of things, have in common?"

Sara sat up a little straighter, taken aback at the unexpected turn in the conversation. "No, Gran. I don't."

"Well, it's that they start out studyin' those things at a real young age. Usually around seven years."

"That's how old I was when you first sent for me," Sara murmured, comprehension beginning to dawn.

"That's right. Gettin' an early start gives you the best chance of fully realizin' your talents, *if* you choose to make your life here. If you *don't* choose to make your life here, then you have to make a clean break. You'd still be young enough to get past the awakenin' of your blood heritage and, in time, you'd forget all about the laputas and everything else, and be able to make yourself a right nice, normal way in the outside world." Gran looked directly into Sara's eyes as though she wanted to make sure there wasn't even a tiny chance of being misunderstood.

"But it has to be a clean break, if you want to follow in your mama's footsteps. Comin' back here just for visits would be unsettlin' and would make it impossible for you to really, truly be a part of either world. You have to commit to one or the other. You have to choose."

"Is that why Mama never talks about you, or Grandpa Cal, or how she grew up?" Sara asked.

"Yes, child. Your mama, my Claire-Anne, wasn't as gifted as you are. She made her choice after seein' the laputas, but not any of the other things you've been witness to. And it was partly because she'd already met your father. She loved him from the start. Loves him still." Granny shook her head, but a wistful smile lingered on her weathered face.

"So that's why Mama never took us to see you or talked about you or did *anything* to remember you by?" Sara sounded indignant. How could her mother have sliced Granny so completely out of her life even if she *had* to make such an irrevocable choice? Didn't family count for anything?

"No, child. She didn't follow the learnin', but she keeps somethin' of the bayou with her, with you all, every day." There was a deep glow in Granny's dark eyes as she spoke, but Sara was still puzzled.

"She never told me anything," Sara exclaimed. "I don't get it, Gran."

The corners of Granny's lips twitched upward. Sara realized she was trying hard not to let a full smile overtake her and turn into laughter. At last, she mastered her mirthful impulse and returned her attention to Sara.

"Who was my husband, your granddaddy?" Granny asked.

"Granddad Cal." Sara didn't understand what this had to do with her own mother's abandonment of her birth family.

"But when I do speak of him, when I speak with my heart, what do I always call your Granddad Cal, girl?"

"You say 'my Cal,'" Sara answered. After five years of pretending not to listen to Granny's tales and stories, she was certain of this. "My Cal" was one of the first times she'd heard longing and sweetness in her grandmother's voice.

"And what is your brother's name?" Granny looked far too smug for Sara's liking.

"Michael," Sara replied with just a touch of sibling disgust. In her opinion, her brother was always lording it over her. Not just because he was older, like her sister Amy-Dean, but because he was the only son her parents had. But as soon as she said the name aloud, Sara realized the connection.

My Cal. Michael.

Her mother had named her only son in honor of her own father, but she had done it in a hidden, secret sort of way.

Sara's breath caught. "Mama never told us," she said, a soft wonder drifting through her words.

"No," Granny affirmed. "She wouldn't bring *this* world, *my* world, so much out into the open."

Sara noted her grandmother's glance had reverted to its usual hard, piercing intensity.

"But there are any number of ways your mama pays tribute to her background. You'll never know the half of them, even if you choose to follow her. And if you choose to follow *me*, you won't learn them either, 'cause you'll be cutting off your ties with that part of your upbringin.'"

Sara's thoughts were ricocheting from question to question, from worry to worry. She felt as though panic wasn't far off. And panic never helped, no matter what the situation. Then something occurred to her that she thought might disprove Granny's assertion that she'd have to abandon one side or the other of her life.

"Wait a minute, Gran," she said, casting a sharp look at her. "If I choose to keep visiting, I'll be *visiting*. I won't be moving out here. So how does that fit in with everything you've been telling me?" She hoped it didn't sound as though she were accusing her grandmother of being shifty, but at the moment, in her present unsettled state of mind, all Sara knew was that something didn't quite add up.

Granny sighed, but didn't sound impatient or offended by Sara's suspicious query.

"You're still very young, child," she explained. "There are still so many things you need to learn from your parents, from your birth family's life and ways. Those things will form the base of how you react and how you behave for the rest of your life. They're a large part of who you are, no matter where you end up or what you end up doing. Basic things like social skills and school lessons are best handled by others than an old granny, who's so out of touch.

"But make no mistake, girl. You'd still be *visitin'* for several years. And each time you return to your home, your life will become more and more difficult. It'll be unpleasant for you, and hard for the others in your life as well. It'll be 'specially painful for your parents to watch you become less and less one of them, to belong less and less in their world, less and less able to have the kind of life most parents hope and assume their young'uns will have.

"So, yes, you're right. You won't be movin' out here all at once, but you will be movin' out eventually. If, for some reason I can't imagine, you change your mind along the way and want to follow in your mama's city ways, it'll be well nigh impossible to have a normal life out there. By then, the swamp-craft and the Power in your blood will own you. You'll never belong anywhere but here and you'll suffer for it." Granny stood, stretched, and took stiff steps toward the front door.

At the threshold, she looked back at Sara. "Any more questions, or are we done for now?"

Through Sara's fretful anxiety, something she'd wondered about for years in idle moments when she was at her parents' home worked its way to the forefront of her thoughts. She twisted around to confront her grandmother's mixed expression of sadness and patient concern.

"Yeah, just one more thing, Gran. Every time there's a hurricane or a big storm, I always wonder how you're getting by. I asked Mama a couple of times, but she always avoided talking about you or this place. And the thing is, she didn't seem worried either. What's it like out here during the really bad storms?"

Granny ducked her head and smiled for the second time that day. Her amusement puzzled Sara.

"Oh, child," she chuckled, "don't you know yet? This place isn't in the same part of the world as your family lives in. No one wanders in here by mistake. The Source has a way of only lettin' in folks who belong, folks it calls. Those tornadoes and hurricanes you hear about might be because the Source is out of balance, but they don't come far into *this* world."

Sara frowned, confused.

"Why do you think your mama doesn't come out to the cabin with you even for a short visit? Why do you think she always stands on the shore and waves goodbye?"

Sara had wondered about that, too. "I figured she didn't like the boat, or maybe she didn't want you to have to row her all the way back, or maybe she didn't want to get caught driving back home so late," she ventured, a little exasperated that she hadn't ever asked. She'd been so self-centered, so caught up in the childish tragedy of having to spend two weeks without blogs, or tweets, or music, or TV or her comfortable, familiar bedroom. Granny's look of reproach told her she was probably thinking the same unflattering things about her.

"No, child. She *couldn't*." Granny turned and walked into the kitchen. Her voice drifted back to Sara with her final words. "Your mama can't come here anymore. Because once upon a time . . . she *chose*."

23

DINING WAS A solemn affair that evening.

Sara could tell Granny had gone to some trouble to make her last supper for this visit special, or maybe it was her last supper here *ever*, depending on the dreaded choice. Granny had pulled up a net that she'd flung off the back porch early that morning while Sara was still asleep. The succulent catfish and crawdads caught within it had been prepared with extra attention to the herbs and spices Sara had learned to appreciate. Crispy cornbread smothered with honey, stewed greens with wild mushrooms, and a vanilla pudding topped with caramelized nuts completed the meal.

When they had finished, the dishes were cleaned, dried, and stacked away in thoughtful silence.

Afterward, as usual, Granny took her seat on the front porch in her rustic, wooden rocking chair. Sara brought in the dry laundry and packed for her departure the next day. Whether she was doing so to have more time in the morning to say farewell to the places she was fond of, or if she was doing so to make a quick getaway, even she didn't know.

When all the little tasks of leave-taking were done, she went out to her grandmother and sat down in what she considered "her" place; the top porch step, with her back resting against one of the pillars supporting the overhanging roof. Sara watched the clay amulets with their strange carvings that hung from the rafters sway in the faint breeze. As darkness fell, she noted the sparkling phosphorescence, which she had so recently discovered, began to appear.

"Will you be mad at me if I don't come back, Gran?" she asked in a small, hesitant voice, gazing into the night, not looking at her grandmother. "Will you hate me?"

Silence reigned for a few moments.

"No, girl," came the soft reply. "I won't think ill of you in any way, but I will miss you sorely." Granny continued to rock, making a soothing, rhythmic, creaking sound. "It will mean the end of our line." She sighed. "If you have a child, I don't expect I'll be around by the time she's old enough to visit here. She won't get to make any choice at all, at all."

Sara leaned her forehead against her palms and closed her eyes. "Granny, I'm not ready. Whatever I choose, I don't know what'll happen."

"Oh, child," Granny whispered in a voice as light as the coolness of the breeze across the water at day's end. "You'll *never* know what's in store. No one does. Your eyes are open. Your mind is open. Now open your heart and follow it. *Wherever* it leads you."

Sara didn't know how long she kept silent, bowed head cradled in her hands, but when she straightened up, deep night, festooned with glowing, enchanted shades of green, lay over the land before her. Granny had gone in, leaving Sara to make up her mind in privacy. But Sara didn't seem able to follow any of her thoughts to a clear end.

She rose and crossed the plank flooring to stand in the cabin doorway. Inside, the lamps were lit, bathing the interior in a warm, honeyed gold. Granny was rustling about in a dusky corner, methodically taking items out of an ancient trunk, inspecting each and then stacking them with care on the floor. She was already surrounded by a collection of curious shapes only half-revealed in the kerosene light. She paused when she saw Sara hovering.

"Gran, I need to think. I'm going for a walk, okay?"

"Of course, child. Just don't go too far. You can't sleep in tomorrow or your mama will be worried waitin' for us." Granny turned back to her exploration of the trunk's contents.

Sara watched her for a moment, and then reached in to lift her jacket from the gnarled, wooden hat tree. She shrugged into the garment, now much the worse for wear after her excursion to the Muckles' shack, went down the steps, and entered the night-lit swamp.

24

WALKING WITH NO clear destination in mind, Sara became entranced by her own footsteps; by the ground passing beneath her feet. As she looked down, an emerald shimmer would radiate out a few inches from wherever she stepped, doing a slow fade as she moved on. She was sure the night glow was stronger than ever before.

I wonder if it's always been like this. Or maybe it really is getting stronger, or the change is in me, and I'm the one who's getting stronger. She couldn't help imagining how her sensitivity might increase if she continued to spend time with her grandmother.

Gazing at her own feet assured her a safe path when it came to stepping into boggy spots or tripping over obstacles like twisted roots or mischievous vines, but it didn't keep her apprised of anything that might be hanging down from overhead. Sara felt something pliant, yet roughly textured, slap against her lowered head with a damp thud. With a grunt of disgust, she froze in her tracks. Instantly aware that whatever had draped itself over her scalp remained still as only an inanimate object could, she batted it away. She wiped her hands on her jeans and was dismayed when the thing swung back, this time hitting her squarely in the face.

"Oh, for Pete's sake." Sara's exasperated voice sounded overloud against the muted background noises of the swamp at night. Meditative walk interrupted, she retreated several steps, peering up at whatever had accosted her. The first thing she noticed was that no greenish luminescence outlined it. *So it's not growing plant life. It's not a natural part of the swamp.* The next impression was the shape of the thing as it hung suspended before her, backlit by the living, phosphorescent, bayou glow. Thick strands were joined together, leaving vaguely rectangular spaces between them. Sara blinked several times as the pattern finally registered through her surprise at seeing something so . . . so regimented.

"It's a *net*," she murmured in disbelieving recognition. Furthermore, there was something glinting, faintly reflective either embedded in the strands of material or fastened to them. As Sara moved her head from side to side, trying to get a better idea of the structure of the thing in the dim light, she realized that the shiny bits were sporadic, placed at the corners of the rectangular spaces.

She grabbed the bottom edge of the woven strands and yanked downward, trying to bring it closer to her eyes for inspection . . . and immediately regretted having done so as the entire net plopped over her. Spluttering, she flailed about until she'd managed to free herself. The net lay in a limp heap before her. She hitched her jacket, which had slipped a bit, back up onto her shoulders and looked about to see if her struggles had been witnessed by anyone or anything. *Anyone who might have set such a clumsy trap.* She couldn't deny the Muckles flashed across her thoughts.

Sara realized she had wandered back to the edge of the clearing where she'd first encountered the swamp-jenny and her tribe. With a soft exhalation, she was struck once again by how lovely this particular little grotto looked at night.

Enchanting, she thought, deciding it really was the only adequate word to describe the beauty before her. She recalled the little swamp sprite and its game of "bubble-splash," wondering if she'd ever get the opportunity to be that close to the elusive creatures again. All the legend and lore that Granny had related to her about the jennies and jacks came to mind. Slowly, a suspicion began to form.

Sara looked at the lumpy mass of crude netting piled at her feet, the bits of material embedded in the fibrous strands catching the light and sparkling even in the dim night glow. She remembered Granny telling her how the swamp-jennies and swamp-jacks found anything bright and shiny irresistibly attractive. And then she recalled having seen something similar. When she had been mesmerized by the odd flow of images deep in the recesses of Froggy's eye, one of the most distinct and disturbing had been a structure like this net. It had begun as a small mesh glittering and undulating, but had swiftly grown large. It had filled the entire field of vision, becoming blurred and huge, then fading and giving way to other shapes and shadows.

Sara regarded the lumpy mass at her feet with distaste. *If what I saw were memories . . . experiences . . . then . . .* She was almost certain that this was how Saylish and Malora Muckle had trapped Froggy in the first place. It was probably how they had planned to enslave other hapless souls as they traveled toward the Source or waited for the serpentrees to find them, unaware that such a devious trap lay in wait to divert them.

Sara thought it also gave credence to her belief that Froggy might have been the soul of a swamp-jenny or jack. If it was legendary that the creatures favored shiny, bright trinkets, she could well imagine that their souls would, by nature, wander toward a glittering temptation trailed across their path.

And then they're caught. Sara toed the net, her disgust with the Muckles reaching new levels of outrage. *How could they? And how did the net get here . . . this close to home . . . anyway? Wouldn't something like this best be used in the river?*

With the realization that the contraption likely had been transported from the waterway populated by strange, pastel lozenges that Granny had shown her, Sara turned her attention to her surroundings once again. It was now eerily quiet. Water and breeze provided the usual background of gentle sound, but Sara heard nothing to indicate the movement of living things. Usually, there was always *something*, if she listened and concentrated hard enough. She scanned the clearing from side to side and from top to bottom. A chill shivered its way down her spine and lifted the tiny hairs on her arms and neck.

I'm being watched, she thought. *They're here. They're watching to see what I do. Did they bring this here? A trap for them, but a test for me?*

It felt as though the entire bayou and all its denizens were waiting for her to do something. Somehow, it seemed vital to demonstrate that she was separate, distinct, *different* from the Muckles and their cruelty.

Sara knelt beside the collapsed net. She felt around the ground and found what she sought: a small, sharp stone. She took it in a firm grip, spread a section of the net before her, and gave vent to her rage, pounding the fibrous strands, trying to severe them. When she hit one of the shiny bits, it shattered with a satisfying crunch. Encouraged by the sense of accomplishment the brittle sound gave her, Sara began a systematic crushing of each fragment of the glittery substance. During the next hour, she worked her way through the entire net. At one point she realized she was accenting her efforts with angry, guttural exclamations, sounding like an enraged mother bear she had once heard on a television nature program.

By the time she stopped, Sara's arm was limp, the muscles announcing their over-use with a strange sensation that felt as though the limb were rising on its own. She leaned back on her heels, releasing her stone weapon. Her hand was stiff and sore. She looked at the patches of powdery shimmer that were all that remained of the net's ornamentation. Sifting some of it through her fingers, she grimaced in recognition.

Mirrors! They broke up a mirror and wedged the shards into waterlogged rope.

Sara's smile was grim. *I really hope that old superstition about seven years' bad luck comes home to them. And I can see why they'd sacrifice a mirror if they had one on hand. Who'd want to see faces like theirs every morning?*

She gave a rueful laugh, remembering how she had complained to Granny time after time about needing a mirror. Somehow, it didn't seem so important anymore.

Sara levered herself up, working the stiffness from her knees, and brushed herself off. Specks of mirror-dust and bits of rope fiber fell from her clothing onto the damp ground. She gazed around the grotto once again. Everything remained unnaturally still, but, as Sara took a deep breath and kneaded the soreness out of her hands, she sensed a change in the quality of silence. She didn't feel quite so watched. If she had to put a name to it, she would say the atmosphere was *companionable*, maybe even *supportive*.

Feeling as though she'd earned a break, Sara picked her way to the leaning cypress where the swamp-jenny had once perched and beneath which she herself had tried to make a good impression by returning the silvery leaf-balls it had been throwing. She recognized the limb where she had left an offering of crumpled foil as an apology for startling the little creatures. She sat on the ground, not minding the moisture that would leave damp marks on her jeans. With a sigh, she leaned back against the cypress' trunk, surprised that it still seemed to retain some of the day's warmth.

Letting her head fall backward, Sara relaxed and admired the scene before her.

My night vision is really changing, she mused. *I'm seeing more detail and, I think, more colors?*

The secluded, little grotto looked more than ever like a fairytale setting. Before, Sara had seen mostly the swamp's signature green. There had been variations in shade and tone, but if anyone had asked, she would have said that everything was in the emerald family. Now, green was still the dominant color, but she saw tiny effervescent touches of gold, red, purple, and an elusive blue, so deep it was frequently lost against the darkness, but when it flared into sight, it was like a jewel-toned treat. Sara found her eyes seeking that blue, just to reassure herself that it really did exist, that she hadn't imagined it.

After a while, when the breeze became chilly, Sara knew that the night had passed its mid-point. She closed her eyes for a moment and made a small whimpering sound to herself. In a few hours Granny would row her to meet her mother, and she was no closer to having made any decision about her future. She imagined sleeping in her comfortable bed with all her little luxuries surrounding her. She thought of the pleasures she took for granted; hearing new music for the first time and feeling its melodic message wind its way around her heart, shopping with friends for something silly that they all simply *had* to have, playing soccer with her school team, sitting down to holiday dinners with her family. But those happy gatherings around the table would never include Granny.

Sara opened her eyes and blinked at the spellbinding beauty that had been hidden from her until just a few days ago. She thought of her adventures with the Muckles and Froggy. She had done something important. She had done something on her own and unimaginable to her before coming to the bayou. Here she was special. Here she was gifted.

You're special at home, too, she told herself with a stern, mental shake. *Just in a different way.*

No, a tiny voice argued. *You're ordinary anywhere but here.*

Sara stood up, brushed herself off once again and cast a last, longing look around the grotto.

This is useless, she thought, running her hands through her hair in frustration, scraping it back from her face. She turned away from the old cypress and made her way to the point where she had entered the clearing. *I'm not getting anywhere. I may as well head back.*

As she passed the shredded, ruined net, crumpled into a soggy heap, something hit her shoulder and bounced off to the side of the path. Startled, Sara jumped and then froze her position as she strained ears and eyes to discover what had assaulted her.

Just a few inches from her foot, a lightness, a sparkle twinkled up at her. She widened her eyes. It was a small, silvery orb; its soft gleam beckoning her. With a careful touch, Sara picked it up.

"Oh." She breathed an exclamation of delight. Holding the tiny ball that was the plaything of a swamp-jenny, she turned back to survey the seemingly deserted grotto.

"Thank you," she called. "I don't know if I'll come again, but thank you."

Cradling the little leaf-ball carefully in her hands, Sara walked through the delicately-lit terrain toward her grandmother's cabin and the start of a new day.

Maybe my last day . . .

25

SARA REACHED THE cabin, where a single lamp was still burning on the porch railing, awaiting her return. She picked it up by its rusted handle and held it before her as she lit her way indoors. She noticed that the contents of the trunk Granny had been digging through had been packed away, the trunk pushed back against the wall. In fact, everything looked in order. There wouldn't be much to do by way of preparation before leaving in the morning.

Sara readied herself for a few hours' sleep, each routine given extra attention, since it might be the last time she performed it. She wanted to be aware of every detail of her stay here at her grandmother's place. Granny had told her that if she chose to live a safe, normal life with her parents, she would eventually forget all she'd experienced here. She didn't want that to happen. So she concentrated on just how the water felt that she used from the big barrel on the back porch. How it tasted like earth and sky and the color green all at the same time. She listened to the gentle lap of water caressing the pilings at the rear of the cabin and savored its scent combining both freshness and decay, of small, stagnant pools and the vast, salty ocean all rolled into one distinctive aroma that would always say "Granny's place," if she ever smelled it in the outside world.

Not greeny-damp anymore, the wistful thought came to her. *Granny's place.*

Most of all, Sara admired the night-glitter. As she snuggled beneath her blanket, she tried to keep as much of the outdoors in sight as possible through the small, square windows overlooking the back porch. She was unaware of falling asleep, but for long afterward she would remember that she dreamed of a forest draped and netted with sparkling, multi-colored lights.

Just like Christmas she would think, trying to recapture a dream of peaceful beauty. *Just like the Festival of Lights . . . of lights back home . . . home . . . home . . .*

26

A FEW HOURS later, Sara was awakened by Granny's bustling breakfast preparations. For a moment she lay still, cataloging the vague discomfort in her muscles, particularly her hands. Then the itinerary of the day shouldered its way to the forefront of her mind and any semblance of leisure evaporated.

Sara sat up, her eyes drawn to the view outside the back porch windows despite the fact that night was over. No shimmering colors would be visible until darkness fell again. And Sara knew that no matter what she chose, she wouldn't be here to see the magic happen as the sun set. By the time it did, she would be sitting in her parents' car, on her way home. She'd be listening to her mother chatter about whatever she'd missed in her two-week absence. She'd hear all about how pretty Amy-Dean was getting and how many invitations she had to summer parties and dates. She'd find out what Michael had done this time to either irk Mama and Papa or make them indescribably proud. In short, the same old things would happen that happened every time she came home. The same old, boring things.

The things she loved.

"Get'cha up. Get'cha up." Granny had noticed that Sara was no longer burrowed into the comfort of her bed; no longer a vaguely girl-shaped lump.

Sara couldn't help noticing, though, that the usual cheerful, rousing chant didn't sound quite so energetic this morning.

She's wondering if I've chosen, Sara thought. *And I have no idea what to tell her*. But she kept her worries to herself for the moment, not wanting to spoil what might be her last morning in her grandmother's world, and tried to match Granny's hollow cheer with her own bright "Good morning, Gran!"

"Come on, girl," Granny called. "We've got a ways to go, a ways to row, and your mama will be waitin'." She noticed her grandmother didn't really look at her, didn't meet her eyes.

Sara washed and dressed, then packed her night clothes into her bag and set it in readiness beside the front door. As she dragged a comb through her hair, she once again was mindful of savoring every action and sensation. She took her place opposite Granny at the kitchen table, eggs and toast sending up inviting aromas from the plate placed before her, and took advantage of Granny's lack of eye contact to study her without being noticed.

It was odd, but Sara didn't see the same faded, stringy-haired, elderly woman who had greeted her the very first time Mama had brought her to the shore beyond Chalmette. If anything, Granny looked younger, more vital than Sara thought she should. After all, years had passed since that first visit. If anything, the solitary, rigorous life Granny lived should have taken a toll on her. But as she ate and kept glancing toward her grandmother, she had to admit that Granny's skin looked smoother, more like polished wood than old leather. Sara was surprised to discover Granny's hair wasn't stringy or limp. It shimmered with a soft, slivery glow and, even tucked up in a bun, Sara could tell it was thick and wavy.

Puzzled, she frowned as she spread butter on warm toast.

Is this just another instance of my eyes being open now? Is this how Granny always looked? Sara shook her head in disbelieving denial. *No! That can't be.* She chewed as she grew thoughtful, not really tasting anything while she tried to reconcile the woman across the table with the version she recalled meeting that first time.

"Somethin' wrong with your breakfast, child?" Granny had noticed Sara scowling at her plate.

"No . . . yes . . . well . . . no, not really," Sara spluttered, disconcerted by the interruption to her thoughts. As she stalled for time, Sara placed the wedge of uneaten toast back on her plate and brushed the crumbs from her hands. She stared at her plate and reflected that for some reason she felt shy this morning, inhibited from bombarding Granny with questions that yesterday would have flown from her lips with no thought or preparation. Today, she didn't want to say anything that would discomfit her grandmother, that would leave a bad taste; would leave a bad last impression. She wanted Granny to remember her with fondness, whether it was until next summer . . . or forever.

So Sara was relieved when Granny made the first move, saving her from having to put her indecision into words.

She heard something being pushed across the grainy surface of the table and looked up.

"This is for you, Sara-Jean," Granny said.

Their eyes met for the first time that morning. Granny's glinted with humor and affection. Sara felt some of her apprehension and guilt about her impending choice loosen. Her grandmother's smile was wide and genuine.

"What is it?" She peered with raised brows at the small, wooden box, polished to a dark sheen.

"Land sakes, girl. Never thought you'd be one to waste a question. Open it and find out."

Sara picked up the box, admiring the pattern of wood grain undulating across its surfaces. It felt smooth and worn, as though it had been opened and its contents inspected many, many times for many, many generations. She cradled it in her palm and thought, *Age. I'm holding age in my hand.* She glanced up at Granny once more before lifting the lid. Her breath hitched.

"Oh, Gran, it's beautiful."

Inside the box was a small cushion of what looked like black velvet. Nestled in the center was a ring of braided silver adorned with three tiny, perfect pearls. The metal looked mellow, as though the ring had been worn and cherished by many different hands. The pearls glowed as if lit from within. Sara stared, lost in the loveliness of the jewelry until Granny prompted her.

"Well, it won't bite, girl. Take it out and look at it proper-like."

Sara lifted the ring from its plush bed and gasped when she discovered a hidden feature. The ring was also set with tiny, green stones, but instead of being on the outside of the band where their display would be apparent, they were on the *inside* of the band. They would be invisible once the ring was worn on a finger. Sara held the unexpected gift in her palm and lifted it to eye level as she inspected it for any other surprises.

"Granny, those stones . . . they're on the inside. No one will ever see them. Why?" She looked at Granny.

"Child, I told you about the magic of green, remember?" Sara nodded. "Well, this keeps that magic close to the wearer. Those green stones, a special type of quartz, aren't for boastful show. They're for remembrance. Of here. Of me."

Sara felt stricken, as though all the breath had been frozen inside her. In truth, she was wondering if Granny already knew which path she would select. It was as though she were already saying goodbye.

"But I haven't chosen, Gran." Sara felt a mixture of mournfulness and dread, the conflicts involved in her situation taking their toll. Granny's soft reply and gentle half-smile did little to sooth Sara's anxiety.

"I know that, Sara-Jean, but I want you to keep this. If you come back to me, it'd be yours by rights anyway. If you don't come back, like I'm a-tellin' you, it'll be a remembrance." Granny rose, turned away, and seemed to take an inordinate amount of interest in clearing away breakfast dishes. "Besides," she continued in a stronger, more officious tone, "there's no one else to leave it to no matter where you choose to make your life."

Sara slipped the ring onto the middle finger of her left hand. It fit perfectly. She wasn't sure if she imagined it in the emotion of the moment, but it felt as though a faint quiver of warmth moved across her skin as the green stones slid into place, hidden from view. She cradled the ring-clad hand against her chest and smiled.

"Thanks, Granny," she said around the lump trying to form in her throat. "I'll never forget you. Or here. Or green and what it means to you. What it means to *us*."

Granny cast a look at her that Sara felt was trying very hard to maintain a cheerful aspect. "Time to be goin', girl." She tossed the remark over her shoulder as she dumped a pile of dishes into the big, tin wash bucket. "We don't want to keep your mama waitin' too long. Do what you got to do, and we'll be on our way."

Sara rose, still cradling her hand wearing the precious ring. She walked to the front door. Standing beside her bag, already packed, she gazed out over the land as the early sun coaxed mist from pools and pockets of moisture; gauzy clouds and columns of vapor lifted from the ground and reached skyward.

"I'm ready," she said, knowing full well that she wasn't.

27

HALF AN HOUR later, they were seated in the familiar rowboat, skimming through reeds and hummocks, listening to a symphony of bird calls punctuated by an occasional splash and ripple as various aquatic denizens of the swamp decided *not* to make close acquaintance at this particular time. Sara was silent at first, and Granny respected her privacy, not wishing to intrude on her granddaughter's thoughts by engaging in useless small talk.

Sara trailed her fingers through the murky waters, wondering if any laputa birds would show up. She smiled at the memory of how shocked she'd been to see them, but how their appearance now would be comforting, like an assurance that whatever powers she was developing weren't going to desert her no matter if she never visited the swamp again. As her mind wandered over the last few days' adventures, she realized with a start that she'd forgotten to tell Granny about her encounter with the mirror-woven net and her certainty that it had been employed by Saylish and Malora Muckle to ensnare Froggy.

"Gran, I found something last night when I went for a walk," Sara began, her voice sounding muffled in the misty air.

Granny was immersed in the task of rowing, her eyes darting about as though her vision could penetrate the fogs and currents surrounding them, or as if she could see things hidden from others. Sara had noticed and wondered if it was related to the constant eye movement that marked her grandmother's evening hours spent on the porch gazing into the swamp night. Having experienced radical changes in what she herself could see, Sara was now quite willing to entertain the possibility that the mists, clouds, and water could contain wonders which weren't visible to her yet.

"What would that be, child?" Granny asked, turning her attention back to Sara for a moment before resuming her darting observance of vapor and sea.

"Well, it was sort of a big net with bits of broken mirror embedded in it to make it all sparkly when it moved." Sara related her suspicions about the net's use and her feeling that the swamp-jennies and swamp-jacks had dismantled it and brought it to their little grotto. After describing how she had destroyed the thing's ability to twinkle and lure other glitter-loving creatures into it, Sara fell silent again. She watched Granny row for a few minutes, then impatience and concern pushed her to ask the question on her mind without giving her grandmother any more time to ponder the matter.

"Gran, do you think I'm right? That Froggy was a swamp-sprite's soul? That someone needs to figure out a way to keep the Muckles from doing that again?" Sara waited for Granny's response, fidgeting with the pearl ring on her finger.

"I 'spect you're right, girl," came the laconic reply.

Sara squinted through the thickening mist, feeling perplexed that Granny wasn't more impressed with her recounting of the night's events, or more invested in what it all might mean.

"Granny, what's wrong?" she finally ventured, wincing a little as her voice bordered on a whine. "Did I do something I shouldn't have? Don't you care about stopping the Muckles?"

Granny stopped rowing. Shipping her oars and letting the little boat continue to drift forward, she trained a stern look on her granddaughter.

"Of course I care, child," her voice was low, but sharp, almost harsh. "I care enough to know I've got to let you go. Didn't you understand all that talk, talk, talk we been doin'? You can't take this world, *my* world back with you. If you try and struggle, it'll just make your life outside a misery. Let it go, Sara-Jean. Let that old ring be enough. Let that be all you take with you." Granny took up her oars and resumed the rhythmic dip and pull that glided them along.

"But I *haven't* chosen, Gran!" Sara felt slighted. It felt like when her sister, Amy-Dean, yelled at her to keep out of her bedroom just because she assumed Sara would trespass at the first opportunity, when Sara had absolutely no interest in setting foot past the cloying, frilly, pink threshold.

"Are you sure about that, girl?" Granny's retort cut through her indignation and brought Sara up short.

She bit back the protest that had been on the tip of her tongue and turned instead to stare into the shimmering, gray mist. *Had* she chosen? Did Granny see something in her that told her more about her than she herself knew? As Sara once again delved into all the pros and cons of living in the bayou or living in the city, she became entranced by the tendrils of fog slipping past.

Her eyes unfocused. And, in a heartbeat between then and now, just as with the laputa birds, Sara *saw*.

How could she ever have thought the twisting, vaporous skeins were gray? Her mouth hanging open in amazement, Sara tried to count the colors, but they wouldn't stay still long enough for her to fasten on any particular one. She was also aware of a faint buzzing sound that made her think of thousands of dry, withered insect wings scraping together. Sara squeezed her eyes shut for a moment, then squinted them open to mere slits and struggled to resolve the swirling rainbow mists into separate elements. When she succeeded, her jaw dropped, her mouth forming an "O" of surprise.

Hundreds, maybe thousands, of tiny creatures smaller than gnats were dashing against each other, grabbing and pushing and poking in an incessant aerial battle. Diaphanous wings tinged with color were blurs above their backs. As Sara's vision sharpened, she recoiled. Some of the foggy vapor surrounding them was just what it appeared to be at first glance: nothing more than mist. But every tendril that moved a bit faster, twirled a bit tighter than its neighbors, was composed of what Sara could only describe to herself as warring factions of winged mini-gremlins. As one wisp curled itself closer, right before her eyes, she saw the tiny, crimped, malevolent faces contorted with snarls and grimaces. Sara ducked and dodged, trying to avoid colliding with the shimmering, little warriors darting about her.

"G-Gran!?" Her voice trembled with shocked discovery. "What are these things all around us? Have they always been here? What are they doing? How . . . ?"

"One question at a time, girl. Lord have mercy, we're back to this, are we? Give a body a chance to answer." Granny shook her head in amusement, a faint smile belying any sting her sharp retort may have carried, but when she continued, Sara thought her grandmother's voice sounded a little sad. "They're called wraithflits, girl. And, yes, they've always been 'round, just like the laputa birds have always been 'round. And you can see what they're doin'. They're fightin'. They've been at war for as long as any of us who know the swamp-craft have been 'round."

Sara felt her shoulders bunch into an involuntary hunch as she sought to protect herself from the newly-discovered violence twisting its colorful way through the air. Almost immediately, though, she realized that not only were the wraithflits never colliding with her, or Granny, or the boat, but if she extended a finger to touch them, they contorted away from her. The misty tendrils marking their presence gave way before her movements exactly the way ordinary fog would have fled from the invisible currents created by a solid object moving through the air. Granny observed Sara's tentative attempts to touch the mist.

"Sara-Jean, it's best if you leave them be," Granny said as Sara's efforts grew bolder.

Sara looked up at Granny.

Granny glanced away, focusing on the steady dip and pull of the oars rather than the curiosity in Sara's eyes. "It's best if you don't see anything more, child . . . for now, anyway."

Sara didn't see how she could ignore something so strange and so suddenly revealed in what she'd taken for granted for years. Eyes still fastened on the incessant rainbow melee before her, she thought *This is why Granny's eyes are always darting about. There must be other things I can't see yet in the night sky, too.* She couldn't let this opportunity slip away, not when this might be her last chance to learn more about the wonders she'd never known filled the swamp with odd life.

"But, Gran . . ."

"Land sakes, child." Granny cut her off. "Haven't you been payin' any attention a'tall to what I been tellin' you these last few days?"

"Well, I, uh . . . there's just been so much . . ."

"Yes, there *has*," Granny interrupted once again. "And the time for questions is *done*. It's time to go home." After a moment of silence, she exhaled and continued in a tone of voice that Sara knew meant *be calm, be reasonable, be patient . . .*

"Child, I don't know what your life is like back city-way, but I do know that even if I hog-tied you and blindfolded you so you'd never see anything more 'til you reached your mama, you're goin' to have a mighty rough time of it readjustin'.

Enough is enough, Sara-Jean. You'd best start thinkin' on home-type things. What you're goin' to do first thing when you get there. What you want to eat or who you want to talk to. That'd be best. Enough is enough . . . Enough is enough . . ." Her voice trailed off. She continued rowing, her eyes still darting about, tracking the aerial antics of the wraithflits.

And who knows what else . . . Sara thought.

28

SARA FELT A familiar seed of rebellion sprout deep in her chest.

Well, maybe I can't get any more answers, but no one can stop me from looking. I wonder what else I can see before we reach shore . . .

With surreptitious glances, she watched the swirling rainbow mists, noting that the tiny, winged armies seemed to be battling to keep each one's signature color dominant. Those with wings tinged orange were shoving and punching any hapless greens or violets that chanced to stray over some invisible, territorial line. Pinks and blues were delivering relentless kicks. A group of yellows looked to be launching a fierce attack against a ragged pack of reds who'd already been pushed back by some aggressive purples.

Sara got caught up, mesmerized by the drama for several minutes before pulling her attention away. If this was her last chance to really *see*, then she didn't want to waste it by going into a trance, no matter how fascinating the grim, little wraithflits were.

She trailed one idle hand in the warm water flowing past their boat . . . and frowned. Something was odd. Moving only her eyes from water to oar, Sara watched Granny rowing. She'd always been impressed with her grandmother's strength and endurance. It was no mean feat to propel a boat through waters thick with rushes and aquatic plants for hours at a time, yet Granny appeared to do so with ease. Now that she took notice, Sara was sure that the gentle effort being applied to the oars was barely enough to stir the water, yet they were speeding along at a pace worthy of a champion sculling team.

Sara looked over the side of the boat, trying to see beneath the algae and other tiny life that always floated on the surface. Her stomach twisted with uneasy anticipation; she had a feeling . . . a bayou-feeling . . . that she was about to discover another facet of Granny's strange world.

Something must be carrying us along.

She leaned further over the side, alternating between squinting and trying to achieve an unfocused stare. Nothing. She resumed letting her hand trail through the current formed by their passage and then reached her fingers deeper, hoping touch would reveal what sight did not. Nothing.

"Sara-Jean, what are you doin'?"

Sara jumped at Granny's voice. "Nothing, Gran. Just . . . just thinking."

She pretended to be picking at a flake of paint below the water line on the rowboat, but a prickly feeling made her sure that she wasn't fooling anyone. Nothing ever seemed to escape her grandmother's notice. In an effort to show she really had nothing to hide, Sara pulled her hand back. Placing it on the wooden seat beside her with a studied lack of concern, she contrived an innocent expression and looked straight into Granny's eyes.

Her own grew wide, white-rimmed, at what she saw. She swallowed hard.

Just as she'd become aware of changes in the appearance of her grandmother's skin and hair back at the cabin, Sara now saw Granny's eyes were not the deep black she'd thought. Fiery gold particles floated in the depths, appearing and disappearing like fragments of glitter being tossed by velvety dark waves. Absurdly, a line from Little Red Riding Hood streaked across Sara's shock-muddled thoughts. *Oh, Granny, what big eyes you have!* As soon as she realized the line's fairytale origin, the tension inside her snapped. Sara began chuckling . . . then laughing, and continued for several minutes. The bemused look on Granny's face as she regarded her only served to fuel Sara's hilarity. Finally, her mirth subsided into airy gasps as she tried to catch her breath.

"Child?" The edges of Granny's mouth quirked upward with sympathetic humor. "Child, what's so funny?"

"Nothing, Gran. Really." Sara gazed deep into Granny's eyes once again, unable to tear herself away, yet fully aware that no more answers or explanations would be forthcoming. "Really, Granny, you don't want to know."

The tilt of Granny's head and the quizzical lift of one brow made Sara think that maybe, just maybe, Granny already did. At any rate, Granny didn't pursue the matter. Instead, she shook her head as she murmured, "Oh, girl, you're goin' to have one rough road readjustin' when you get back city-way."

At last, the strangeness and the amount of it she'd had to deal with over the last several days overwhelmed Sara. She stared into the leaky bottom of the boat, letting her mind wander from memorable moment to moment, only sneaking sporadic looks at her grandmother's eyes, her effortless rowing, the bizarre formations of mist, and the inexplicably strong wake of their boat. Her thoughts drifted from tidbits of lore concerning lemon-weed, to Saylish and Malora Muckle's taunts, to the trill of the swamp-jenny's giggle, to the scent of Granny's homemade soap, to the mirror-studded netting glistening in the ephemeral night glow.

Sara mused about mirrors. How something so ordinary could be turned into a trap in the wrong hands; how she'd asked for the use of one so many times when she first began visiting the swamp; how Granny had made a point of refusing to provide one and had even asked Sara not to bring one with her . . . ever. Sara sat up straighter, as another piece of this puzzling world slipped into place. She was just beginning to see and already her grandmother looked so different. Other things looked different, too. And there were no mirrors at the cabin.

Sara's stomach gave a slow roll that had nothing to do with seasickness. She raised her head to look at Granny, at the escaped tendrils of flowing, shining silvery hair, the smooth sculpted skin, the eyes with sparks bubbling up from their depths.

"Gran," she said, voice thick with apprehension, a lump growing in her throat, "What do I look like here? What do you see when you look at me?"

Granny paused in her gentle rowing and smiled. "Enough questions, child." But as she leaned back into the oars, Sara heard her say soft words, as though she were speaking to someone else, someone Sara couldn't see, "There's a certain family resemblance. The girl has my eyes after all. Now hush . . . no more . . ."

29

SARA SPENT THE rest of the journey trying *not* to see. Granny was right. Enough was enough. She had plenty to occupy her thoughts for the rest of the year until . . . *if* . . . she returned. She closed her eyes and touched her hair in a nervous gesture, certain that it had an unfamiliar wave and texture. She stared at her hands cradled in her lap and twisted the pearl ring, heavy on her finger. Every once in a while she felt a prick as though one of the green stones set inside the band were sending her some signal she couldn't interpret . . . *Yet*, she thought.

She glanced at the colorful, swirling mists from time to time, but only to reassure herself that they were still there. Mostly, she wanted comfort. She wanted to be in her own room with Mama cooking one of her special welcome-home meals, and Papa hanging about the kitchen, sharing a glass of wine and joking with his wife. Hearing the murmur of her parents' voices as she lounged on her bed always made Sara feel safe. It made her think she was part of something unchanging. Her family would always be there.

Her brother's image intruded on her. Michael. My Cal.

Sara covered her face with her hands, feeling the unaccustomed ring smooth against her cheek. Nothing would "always be there." Even if she did nothing, if she stayed in her room buried under the covers and refused to go anywhere, or do anything, or make any choice, changes would happen.

Granddad Cal was gone. Someday Granny would be gone. Everyone would move on.

I'm only eleven. I shouldn't have to worry about stuff like this.

Like an echo on the edge of hearing, Sara heard something so deep it was more like feeling than hearing. She couldn't tell if it was her own thoughts, something from within, or something from without.

Worry is useless. A misuse of imagination. Dream. Don't worry. Dream.

Despite her mind being filled with scattered images and troubled thoughts, the steady motion of the boat, the gentle sounds of air and water, and the warm humidity lulled Sara to sleep. She dozed until the boat gave a sharp roll to one side, jarring her awake. She sat up straight, rubbing her eyes and taking stock of her surroundings.

Whatever had been aiding in the boat's progress had apparently abandoned them. Granny was now laboring at the oars with greater effort, pulling them through the weed-filled water.

Sara didn't hear the dry, abrasive rustling that she had associated with the constant wing motion of the wraithflits. She turned her head from side to side, peering at the drifting, writhing mists. No pitched battles were being waged. She thought she saw an occasional stray creature streak past attended by a blur of color, but she couldn't be sure. As she continued to blink and squint, unsure of whether the tiny winged warriors were gone or if she'd lost the power to detect them, Sara noticed that they were moving through a different sort of fog than before. In comparison to the delicate hues of the wraithflits, it looked dank and dreary. Before she could accustom herself to the change, the fog thinned, then dispersed.

Looking ahead, Sara saw the familiar grassy shore where Mama always waved her off and then met her two weeks later.

Shading her eyes against the glare of light on the water, she saw two people standing close together, watching the approach of the little boat. Sara leaned forward, a happy grin lighting her face.

"Granny. Look. It's Mama *and* Papa. They both came."

Granny didn't seem quite as thrilled about the presence of her son-in-law as Sara was. She sighed and continued rowing. "I know, child. I know."

Sara was too excited to wonder how her grandmother could know both her parents were present when she was turned away from them, the bow of their little craft arrowing forward with Granny facing the stern.

As they drew nearer, Sara waved. Her mother's arm lifted high, returning the greeting, but her father didn't. Even from a distance, Sara could tell by his familiar body language that he was peering into the vanishing mist, scanning the marshy terrain from side to side. She could imagine his brow furrowed in concentration. What she couldn't understand was why her mother could see the boat and its occupants, while Papa apparently was having some difficulty doing so.

Still some way from shore, Sara's parents' voices carried across the water. Mama continued to wave with one arm, the other draped easily around her husband's waist.

"There they are. They're coming. Wave, honey." Mama's eyes crinkled with merriment as she encouraged Papa to join in. But Sara watched, puzzled, as her father continued to search.

"I don't see them, Claire. How can you?" His irritation and doubt were plain to hear. Sara saw her mother turn her head toward him.

"For goodness sakes, Matthew. You're looking right at them." She pointed straight at the oncoming rowboat before resuming waving. After a few seconds, Sara was close enough to be able to discern their facial expressions. She was relieved when Papa's brows shot up and a wide grin replaced his frown.

"I see them." He mirrored Mama's pose, waving with one arm and casually hugging her mother with the other. Her mother gave him a sad, resigned glance before turning her attention back to Sara's homecoming.

Granny rowed the boat up to the usual spot where it could be pulled up onto the beach, allowing its passengers to alight without having to wade through mud and water. She shipped her oars and tossed a line fastened to the boat's prow toward Papa. Still grinning, he snatched it out of the air and dragged them to shore.

Sara clambered out, running past her grandmother, who disembarked at a more sedate pace with Papa's hand to help her. She threw herself into her mother's arms, just as she had at the end of her bayou visit for the last five years.

"Oh, Mama," she blurted out, "you won't believe it. I had the *best* time. There's so much to tell you." Her mother's eyes flickered, but Sara didn't notice.

She moved to her father next and gave him a tight hug as well, unaware of the meaningful glances exchanged between Mama and Granny. Unaware, too, of the tension that rimmed her mother's smile.

In the past, every time Sara had returned, her first words had been about how glad she was to be coming home, how relieved she was to have another year's obligatory visit over.

Clearly, this year was different.

30

SARA SNUGGLED AGAINST her father and looked up at him, her nose crinkling the way it did when she was happy. "Papa, I didn't expect you to be here. You never came before. I'm glad."

Her father looked down at her and ruffled her hair. "Hi, Bug," he said, using his pet name for her. "Your mother thought it was important we both be here this time. I'm not sure why, but I went ahead and took the day off to keep her company and . . . to come *bug collecting*!" With a shout, Papa swung Sara up and around as though she weighed no more than a butterfly. It was a move that he'd been doing for as long as she could remember, and she loved it. He finally let her feet touch the ground, and they looked over to where Mama and Granny were talking, heads close together.

Papa took Sara's hand, swinging his arm back and forth which forced a giggling Sara to twist and turn to keep up with his longer limbs and greater height.

"Let's go see what the *big* girls are talking about," he whispered, making it sound like a Top Secret conspiracy.

Still holding hands, they strolled over to where Granny and Mama were deep in discussion. But as they came within hearing range, both Sara and her father felt their smiles fade. Even before they could separate out any exact words, it was obvious from the harsh, staccato tones and gestures that an argument was in progress.

"Well, didn't take you two long to lock horns, did it?" Papa tried to lighten the atmosphere with a forced smile as he and Sara came to stand beside Mama.

Sara felt as though by standing next to her parents and facing Granny, she was taking sides. It made her uncomfortable, so she squirmed her hand out of her father's grip and stepped a little forward and to the side so she was midway between what felt like opposing forces.

"Hello, Matthew." Granny's tone was cordial as she took a moment to look at the son-in-law she'd only seen a handful of times in the past when he'd become enamored of her daughter and had made it clear he intended to spirit her away from the bayou to be his bride. "It's been a long time. How are you?"

"Hello, Abra-Lynn. I'm good . . . You look well."

Sara was surprised that, although her father's tone wasn't hostile, it was quite frosty. She'd grown up accepting the fact that her mother's side of the family consisted of only one person who was chronically absent. This was the first time she'd realized that this oddity might be a source of resentment for Papa. Feeling nervous, Sara reached up and tucked a strand of hair behind her ear. As she did so, the ring Granny had given her caught the sun, its pearls glowing like cream against the dark of her hair.

Mama noticed the jewelry instantly.

"That's a pretty ring. Where did you . . . ?"

The words died. Looking perplexed, Mama fell silent. She took hold of Sara's wrist, bringing the ring closer for inspection. After regarding it from different angles, she released her daughter's hand and frowned.

"Something about . . . I think I've seen . . ." Mama looked at Granny. "*Have* I seen that ring before, Mom?"

Sara studied her grandmother's face. She didn't think she'd ever seen such an expression of sad, grim composure.

"You've *worn* that ring before, Claire-Anne."

The two women locked eyes long enough for Papa and Sara to feel uncomfortable, as though they were standing on the edge of something they weren't meant to be part of. Sara fidgeted, twisting the ring in question around and around her finger.

"Well, Bug, that's some present your grandmother gave you." Her father turned his attention to Granny. "I'm not sure she should accept it, though, Abra-Lynn. It looks valuable. Might be too much for just a kid. Everything she's into, she might lose it or damage it. Maybe you should save it for her until she's older?" He looked hopeful, and Sara could tell he was trying to be diplomatic and defuse a situation that he really didn't understand.

"She takes it now or she doesn't take it at all," Granny said with more dignity and finality than Sara had ever heard her use before, even when lecturing or telling tales about the ancient heritage that she hoped to pass on to Sara.

Papa chewed on his lip and looked at the ground, digging at a clump of soil with the toe of his shoe.

"Not to be rude, but I don't get it." He looked up and glanced between his wife and mother-in-law. "There's no reason you can't save that ring and give it to Sara when she comes back next summer. Or the summer after that. Or maybe just once come and visit *us* and bring it with you? We'd love it if you'd come and stay with us, Abra-Lynn. Why, you've never even met our other children." Sighing, Papa gave his head a shake. "No reason you can't give her that ring another time."

"Yes there is," Granny declared. Her eyes moved to Mama's face. "*You* understand, Claire-Anne. Even if you've forgotten almost everything, you haven't forgotten *that*."

Sara's mother looked pale, lips compressed into a thin line. "I know, Mom. I know." Her voice sounded weak and thready. She straightened. Her daughter's future was at stake and maternal instinct strengthened her. "Things aren't as simple as when I was Sara's age, Mom."

"Oh, yes they are, girl," Granny interrupted. "Even simpler. The world is maybe more perilous and danger-some than back then. That only means it needs the likes of us . . . the likes of *her* that much more."

"But I don't want her to miss out on a normal life. I don't want it to end up we just see her once a year for a few minutes on this shore. I want her to be part of our family like a regular person, not some hermit we tell stories about each holiday so we won't forget we ever knew her." Mama's eyes filled with tears that spilled their way down her cheeks.

Papa put his arm around her shoulders and cinched her in close to his side, trying to comfort and protect without a clear idea of what was so distressing. He turned eyes that were beginning to sparkle with anger on his mother-in-law.

"Abra-Lynn, we'll bring Sara back next year, same as always."

"*Not* same as always, Matthew." Granny's voice was low and clipped, indicative of her own burgeoning anger. "She's already changed." Granny turned to Sara's mother. "She saw the birds, Claire-Anne. And not just the birds, but so much more. So much more that at times it took the starch right out of me."

"Birds . . . ?" Sara's mother looked confused, her brow creased in an effort to understand, to connect the pieces of what Granny was trying to tell her.

Sara couldn't remain a spectator any longer. Her eyes glittered with excitement.

"Yes, Mama. Birds. The laputas. They were going so fast and there were so many of them. They flew right by me under the water, and I guess they were always there, but I never *saw* them before." The wonder of the experience was still fresh in Sara's mind and carried into her voice. "Oh, Mama, they were so, so . . . *strange!*" She trailed off at the look of disbelief on her father's face and the shock that glazed her mother's.

"Oh, come on, Bug," Papa scoffed. "Are you sure it wasn't just a school of fish? There are tons of them out there. All different kinds."

"No, Papa. No. There were feathers. And beaks. And wings, not fins. I'm sure. And . . . and I could hear them; a kind of humming, clicking that fish don't make."

"Laputas . . . laputas . . . *under* the water . . ." Mama closed her eyes and swayed within the support of her husband's arm. "*Under* the water . . ." She shuddered.

"Honey, are you okay?" Papa bent his head to look into Mama's face.

Just as the other three were beginning to exchange uneasy glances, Mama straightened, opened her eyes and took a deep breath. She gazed out over the water.

"I don't really remember," she said more to the strange land lying beyond the lingering mists, than to her family. "But I guess I do understand. I just don't want to lose my youngest, my baby." She turned tragic eyes to her husband. "Matthew, before I said I'd marry you I explained about my people, my ancestors. You knew then that my choice wasn't easy. I've forgotten so much, but I know there's something waiting out there. And if Sara-Jean wants it, we can't stop her." Unfettered tears slid down Mama's cheeks, but her voice was firm, unwavering.

"You *can* stop her," Granny chimed in, "but you'll destroy her if it's against her will. She'll never forgive you and you'll still lose her, sure as sure."

"Oh, for Pete's sake," Papa muttered. "You told me some superstitious folk tales, Claire. This is all a bunch of nonsense." He dropped his arm from his wife's shoulders and made a dusting motion with his hands, as though brushing them clean of something unpleasant. "You womenfolk have gone too far. It's great to have family stories and traditions, but you're not going to scare me with them and you're not going to enslave my daughter to them."

He drew himself up, giving Granny a courteous nod. "Abra-Lynn, it's nice to see you again. I hope someday you decide to come visit us. It'd be a shame to miss out on knowing the rest of your family just because of some foolish fairytales." Papa turned his back on the three generations of women and stalked back toward the family car parked on a gravel patch at the end of the road.

"He doesn't understand and he never will," Granny said, shaking her head as Papa walked away, his shoulders stiff with discomfort.

Mama covered her mouth with one hand and tried to control her tears. "Oh, Sara," she breathed, voice trembling with emotion. Sara couldn't tell if it was fear or sorrow. "Oh, Sara-Jean, think of how wonderful your life will be when we get home. You'll have all your friends and all the things you love to do. In a few years you'll get to go to college or a trade school. You'll know better then what you really want to do with your life and you can study and learn and find others who share your interests.

"And one day you'll meet someone who it feels like you've been waiting for, and you'll marry and have children and . . . oh . . . so many *wonderful* things. That's what I want for you, Sara. That's what I've dreamed about for each of my children since the day they were born." She ended on a dry sob.

"That's all well and fine, Claire-Anne, but all I'm a-hearin' is what *you* want." In the strange, flat light reflected from the water, Granny looked different. For a moment Sara thought she was watching a confrontation between her mother and some creature carved from shell, glowing with an inward power that made her mother's concerns seem fleeting and inconsequential.

Sara shook her head, breaking the spell by glancing down at the ring on her finger; concentrating on its design. *I never did ask if these were cultured or freshwater pearls*, she thought. *I wonder which . . .*

She looked back up at her mother and grandmother, hoping they'd come to an agreement, or at least a truce soon. They were still facing each other, Mama with her arms folded across her midriff as though protecting herself or holding something in so it wouldn't escape. Granny's voice remained firm and clear.

"We all know what *you* want, Claire-Anne. But what does Sara-Jean want?"

Minutes passed.

Granny's eyes remained fixed on her own daughter. "Ask her, Claire-Anne. Ask Sara. It's time."

31

MAMA TURNED HER head toward Sara. Face oddly blank and slack, she stared at her daughter as though seeing a stranger, someone she'd never met before. Sara shivered and took a step back. But then Mama's eyes stopped her.

"Sara-Jean Mayhew," she said with ritualistic solemnity. "Where will you live in years to come? I am your mother. It is my place to ask you. I, and the women of your line, ask you to choose." There was something of green in Mama's eyes; so much forgotten, but the words passed down from mother to daughter were cell deep.

The moment she had dreaded was upon her. Sara looked from Mama to Granny and back again. She dropped her gaze to the ground, twisting the ring on her finger. Thoughts and images raced through her, reminding her of what she'd seen flashing past when she'd been mesmerized, looking into Froggy's eye.

On the one hand she saw a pastel, hazy world of comfort and security. The smiling faces of her friends and family, moments of love and joy intermingled with occasional sorrow and loss; the feeling of being enveloped in a warm, toasty blanket of acceptance, of belonging, of being *normal*. It felt safe and seductive. Sara closed her eyes and smiled. How lovely it would be to do what her mother wanted; what her father expected.

Her smile faded.

The other world that beckoned was filled with darkness and strange encounters, but it also held breathtaking, indescribable beauty. There would likewise be moments of love and joy, sorrow and loss, but they would be touched with unexpected magic. She might have important things to accomplish in either world, but the circumstances would be quite different. Accomplishment in Mama's world would be recognized and lauded by family and public.

But what I do in Granny's world would have more effect on everyone. It would be so much more important. But almost no one will know what I do. No matter which world I end up in, I'll fade from the other. After a while, I won't matter. So I better do what matters to me, *not anyone else. Not Granny. Not Mama. Not Papa. Me. Only me . . .*

Something splashed among the tussocks out in the marsh. Sara looked toward the sound. The fading mists were still writhing, forming twisted, vaporous sculptures as though reluctant to leave until something was decided. She thought for a moment that one column of mist shimmered with hues of purple and orange, wrapping around itself in a tiny-winged battle.

What do **I** *want?*

Sara took hold of the ring and moved it toward the knuckle as though about to remove it. It felt strangely heavy. She closed her eyes and waited for a sign, something to tell her what to do.

She gasped.

The darkness behind her eyelids was green. Undeniably, spectacularly green.

Sara took a deep breath and looked up at her mother and grandmother watching, expectation and dread in both their faces.

"I'm sorry," she said, her voice soft. "I'm sorry." She looked into her grandmother's black eyes brimming with ancient wisdom; vagrant sparks of gold drifting through their dark depths. "I choose . . ."

Sara's throat was dry. She swallowed what felt like all the feelings in the world.

"I choose you, Granny. I want to learn more. I have to. I'm so sorry, Mama." The weight of her words, the tension that they released within her was too much. Sara covered her eyes and sobbed.

"Oh, Sara . . ." Her mother's strangled moan was muffled as she, too, buried her face in her hands.

"I'm sorry, too, Claire-Anne," Granny whispered.

Sara looked up and saw a triumphant kind of hope and relief glowing in her grandmother's quiet smile.

Granny touched Sara's cheek. "I'll be seein' you next summer, girl." Her grin broadened. "And someday not too long away you'll see the swamp in winter. Wait'll you see the wraithflits all frosty-bright and spinnin' . . . it's quite somethin'."

"I'll be there, Gran." Sara blinked back her tears and swallowed her welling emotions. Now that the decision had been made, she felt a lightness where terrible doubt had been. She was free. Free to see what waited for her and how she would change as she grew and learned the swamp-craft.

She looked at her mother and tried not to feel as though something now lay between them: a crack, a difference, a separation. She told herself that Mama seemed more resigned than defeated; that this was how things were supposed to be.

Mama took Sara's hand and gave a little tug. "It's time to go."

She didn't say it was time to go home. Home would be a different place for Sara from now on. The separation had begun.

Giving Granny a lingering, mournful look, Mama nodded and managed a sad, twitching of her lips that was meant to be a smile. "Bye, Mom. See you next year." Maintaining her grip on Sara, she turned and walked back to where Papa was leaning against the hood of their car, waiting. Just before they reached him, Sara's mother turned back.

"I love you, Mom," she called.

Mist seemed to be flowing in from the bayou once more, obscuring the old lady and her rowboat.

"I love you, too, Claire-Anne." The response drifted back to them through the thickening fog.

At the last minute, just before taking her usual place in the back seat of the car, Sara remembered something; one last question . . . a minor one, so Granny shouldn't mind. She stepped back from the open car door and held her hand wearing the ring toward the fading figure of her grandmother.

"Thanks, Gran! Thanks for everything . . . and thanks for the ring! Freshwater pearls, right?"

Laughter fluttered through the fog.

"Land sakes, girl. Those aren't pearls. They're polished bone. Pearlized, right enough, but that's what happens to bones if'n they're out bayou-way long enough."

Sara stared at her hand. *Whose bones? How . . . ?*

"Come on, Bug. Get in the car." Papa was already behind the wheel and Mama was settling herself in the front passenger seat. Sara clambered into the back. Kneeling on the cushioned seat, she gazed through the rear window to where Granny stood, watching their departure through the thickening mist.

As they pulled away, Sara waved for as long as she could still discern the old lady standing at the water's edge. She didn't see the grim look that settled on Papa's face . . .

. . . or the pallor of Mama's . . .

. . . as white as pearlized bone.

Cat Jenkins has had short stories in horror, fantasy, speculative fiction and humor published. With a checkered career in theatre, ballet, television and radio that took her from coast to coast, from L.A. to NYC, Cat Jenkins now lives in the Pacific Northwest, where the weather is often conducive to long hours before a keyboard. *Sara When She Chooses* is her first novel.

CPSIA information can be obtained
at www.ICGtesting.com
Printed in the USA
FSHW01n1923061018
52727FS